"At the count of three let the exchange begin."

The German terrorist counted aloud and when he reached three, Karl Hahn and David McCarter slowly started walking toward each other.

"The exchange of prisoners has begun," Beck informed Katz and James, who were hiding in the back of the van. "Get ready."

"Got it," James whispered, holding his weapon in his left hand, while gripping the handle of the van's sliding door in his right. "Just give me the word."

McCarter and Hahn were within ten feet of each other, separated by the brick barbecue. It was there that McCarter would pass his M-11 to—

A sudden crack of rifle fire broke the mounting tension. Something slammed into McCarter's chest, throwing him to the muddy ground. Pain enveloped the Phoenix Force warrior and his world turned black.

Mack Bolan's
PHOENIX FORCE

PHOENIX FORCE

The Bonn Blitz

Gar Wilson

A GOLD EAGLE BOOK FROM
WORLDWIDE

TORONTO • NEW YORK • LONDON • PARIS
AMSTERDAM • STOCKHOLM • HAMBURG
ATHENS • MILAN • TOKYO • SYDNEY

First edition July 1987

ISBN 0-373-61330-X

Special thanks and acknowledgment to
Paul Glen Neuman for his contribution to this work.

Printed in Canada

PROLOGUE

The animals had been fed.

The routine never varied. Three times a day Rudolf Schall made his rounds, delivering meals prepared in the prison kitchen to the select group of prisoners incarcerated in the maximum security wing. As a trustee and a senior resident of Stuttgart's Stammheim Prison, Schall had been making his rounds for nearly fifteen years.

Tonight's supper was meat pie and fresh vegetable soup, not one of Schall's favorite combinations—and he had tasted them all. The food would be delivered hot, but Schall took no responsibility for its quality.

The convicts who passed as cooks in the kitchen were impostors. Where the meat for the pies had come from was anyone's guess. And as for the fresh vegetables in the soup, Schall supposed they must once have grown in the soil, but after they'd been canned or frozen and thawed, overcooked, stored as leftovers and resurrected for soup, no farmer would have recognized them.

Pushing his cart slowly along his route, Schall was in no particular hurry to complete his evening rounds. Doing so would only find him unloading dirty trays in the kitchen, and then returning to his cell for the rest of the night. At least while he pushed his cart with its squeaking wheels to and from the kitchen he could entertain the illusion of being a free man again.

Through the years such illusions had become important to Schall. The mind games kept him sane. He would be a guest at Stammheim until the day he died, but by imagining the joys of freedom, he kept himself from going mad.

One day he might pretend to be a farmer feeding his chickens, while the next he would be a sea captain throwing food overboard to the whales. Today he was a zookeeper bringing dinner to the hungry animals in their cages. Of all the roles Schall played, that of zookeeper was the closest to his heart.

"Back so soon?" a uniformed guard asked as Schall and his cart approached the final barrier separating the maximum security wing from the rest of the prison. "Mustn't give the beasts time to dirty their cages, is that it?"

"Animals will be animals," Schall answered cheerfully in return, silently grateful that the young guard chose to humor him. "Besides, you know how restless my pets become whenever I am late to say goodnight."

"Of course, Schall," the guard said, sliding open the barred door for him to pass. "Watch your step."

"Thank you."

Schall pushed his cart through and did not look back when the guard shut the door with a metallic clang behind him. For the next ten minutes the zookeeper was on his own, and Schall was determined to enjoy himself.

His first stop was the cell of Hermann Meier. An outwardly gentle man with sad drooping eyes and slumped shoulders to match, Meier had an uncontrollable temper that had claimed the lives of his wife and her lover, and of three inmates soon after Meier had arrived at Stammheim. Incarcerated in the maximum security wing for his own protection, as well as for the safety of his fellow prisoners, Meier was invariably courteous to Schall.

Schall, the zookeeper, saw Meier as a big bear whose only flaw was letting his emotions govern his actions. It was a character trait Schall understood only too well.

"So, how was supper this evening?" Schall asked as Meier dutifully pushed his empty tray through the slot in the cell door provided for that purpose. Automatically Schall took an inventory of the articles on the tray: one soup bowl, one spoon, one fork. Knives were not permitted in the maximum security wing. Schall placed the tray and its contents on his cart, then said,

"The meal seems to have agreed with you well enough."

Meier's shoulders rose and fell. "It will be a miracle if I'm still living by morning," he said. "What kind of experiments are the cooks performing on us anyway? I know we have no choice but to eat what they dish up. Still, it's a crime, Schall. A real crime. The cooks break the law with each meal they fix."

"Yes," Schall said, beginning to push his cart to the next cell on his route. "If it's any consolation to you, Meier, I happen to know that the cooks eat the same food they prepare for the rest of us."

"And they probably enjoy it, too," Meier grumbled, turning away. "They're not cooks—they're masochists. See you in the morning, Schall. Bring a good breakfast."

"I'll see if I can get you some leftover meat pie."

Meier did not look back. "Don't do me any favors."

A moment later Schall picked up the tray, bowl and cutlery of a retired bank robber named Wiess. A short, fat man, Wiess reminded zookeeper Schall of a walrus.

Altogether there were more than a dozen cells for Schall to visit, including those of a tiger, a monkey and a horse. As he had done when he'd distributed the meals, Schall visited the snake's cage last.

Of all the men imprisoned in Stammheim, Schall disliked the snake the most. During his years at

Stammheim Schall had met them all: murderers, rapists, thieves and con artists. Blackmailers, arsonists, forgers and kidnappers. They were society's outcasts, but Schall could accept them and their crimes.

With the snake it was different. Schall had no compassion for the man called Josef Roetz. Schall could understand crimes stemming from hate and greed; he could understand crimes of passion. But for a man to stoop so low as to sell out his own country to its enemy, to Schall that was the worst crime of all.

Schall had followed Roetz's case in the newspapers he read in the prison library. For more than thirty years Roetz and his family had lived in Bonn, West Germany's capital. Roetz had started his treasonous career as a minor bureaucrat within the *Bundestag*, the Lower House of Parliament, and eventually worked his way up to membership of the *Bundesrat*, or Upper House. There he became a valued and trusted confidant to some of West Germany's highest elected officials.

The whole time, Roetz had been spying for the Russians, feeding the Communists valuable tidbits of information garnered from high-ranking government associates in Bonn, or through contacts established and developed elsewhere, such as in the country's armed forces, the *Bundeswehr*. The number of secrets Roetz had divulged to the Soviets would never be known, nor could the full extent of the damage caused by his traitorous acts be measured.

Had Roetz worked alone? The verdict was still pending on that one, and probably would not come to light until Roetz's trial got under way next month. In the meantime, Roetz was the government's guest at Stammheim.

Success breeds confidence, and sometimes that confidence breeds mistakes. Roetz's undoing had come in the form of a prostitute he saw on a regular basis. She was a very patriotic "lady of the evening." Alerted by comments Roetz allegedly made in the afterglow of their lovemaking, the woman subtly encouraged him to tell her even more. Roetz, the overconfident fool, had done precisely that, supplying enough clues to the true nature of his business in Bonn for the prostitute to take her suspicions to the proper authorities.

Overnight Roetz became a national disgrace, a source of political embarrassment that refused to go away. He had been at Stammheim for almost five months, and even yet the repercussions of his actions were being felt throughout the country.

Schall brought his cart to a stop as he came to the steel door of Roetz's cell. The prison trustee glanced down and frowned. Normally Roetz shoved his empty food tray through the slot in his cell door before Schall requested it. But this time there was nothing.

"Come on. Let's have it." Schall rapped his knuckles against the flat piece of steel that served as a door. "I haven't got all night, Roetz. Give me your tray and be done with it."

Schall beat his knuckles against the door again, then stared at the slot, waiting for the tray to appear.

"No funny business, Roetz," Schall warned, "or tomorrow you get a slice of moldy cheese and cold coffee for breakfast. Do you hear?"

Roetz gave no answer. Schall swore and eased his cart farther along so that he could look into the cell through the square of double-thick glass set into the door at eye level. The snake was lying on his cot with his back to the door. The tray, with its meat pie and vegetable soup uneaten, was in the middle of the floor.

"You're pressing your luck, Roetz," Schall announced. "I'm the guy who feeds you, remember? Screw around with me and you'll starve, I promise."

But Roetz ignored the threat, lying motionless on his side. Schall squinted, his nose flattened against the tiny window. Something was wrong. He reached inside his pocket for his glasses and slipped them on.

"Damn it, Roetz!" Schall complained, looking through the window again. "Get your lazy ass off that cot and bring me your tray. I'm in no mood for..."

Schall's words dried to dust in his throat. For the first time he noticed that Roetz wasn't breathing. Not only that, a dark damp spot stained the pillow just beneath Roetz's head.

There could be no doubt. The damp patch soaking the pillow was blood. The snake was dead.

Rudolf Schall slipped off his glasses and put them away, then turned from the cell and went to find a guard.

1

"We have him now," Georg Ruhl said. "The road our quarry took is a dead end. What a stroke of good fortune."

"A dead end, you say?" Max Fleisch repeated. "How can you tell? All these side roads look alike."

"Not to me they don't," Ruhl insisted. "I've lived in and around Bonn my whole life. I know this region well."

"Where does the side road lead?" asked the vehicle's other passenger from the backseat. "Any place in particular?"

Ruhl flicked his eyes to the rearview mirror before answering. "Just a farmhouse."

"Occupied?" the passenger sitting behind Ruhl wanted to know.

"The last I heard it was empty," Ruhl offered.

"That makes sense," the passenger said. "It's the kind of place Heisler would use for a hideout."

"Whatever he's using the farmhouse for, we've got him," Fleisch said, cranking his window open far enough to flick his cigarette butt into the damp. "If the road's a dead end like Georg says, then Heisler is as good as ours."

The passenger settled back into his seat and left the two men up front to their conversation. Neither Ruhl nor Fleisch cared for him much, resenting that he had been brought in on the case, but the passenger could not have cared less.

Ruhl and Fleisch worked for the Federal Office for the Protection of the Constitution, the *Bundesamt für Verfassunasschutz*, or BfV, which concerned itself primarily with threats to internal security.

A second federal agency, the *Bundesnachrichten-dienst*, or BND, was an intelligence agency and a counterintelligence service, dealing with problems beyond the country's borders that jeopardized the Federal Republic of Germany. The passenger in the back seat was one of the nation's top BND operatives.

From time to time the BfV and the BND found it beneficial to work together on a case, as Ruhl, Fleisch and the BND man were doing in this instance.

The suspect they had tailed from Bonn to the farmhouse road went by many aliases, but his real name was Gunther Heisler. The reason for their following him was his association with one of West Germany's most notorious bands of terrorists.

The late 1960s and the turbulent seventies had spawned a number of left- and right-wing terrorist groups in West Germany, extremists dedicated to making life hell on earth for any who opposed their fanatical beliefs. The undisputed model for these groups was the infamous Baader-Meinhof Gang, which got the terrorism ball rolling in 1968 with bank robberies, bombings and murders. Newspaper headlines soon made the groups household names: Baader-Meinhof, the June 2 Movement, the Red Army Faction and others.

Responding to public outrage that such atrocities were going unpunished, a government-endorsed crackdown eventually put most terrorist groups out of commission. Many extremists were killed in clashes with the authorities. Others were tried for and convicted of their crimes and sentenced to lengthy prison sentences. A scattered few disappeared from sight and were never seen or heard from again.

But for every group that ceased to exist another equally as dangerous was poised offstage, waiting to perform in the arena of hate and despair cultivated by its predecessors. Gunther Heisler and his barbaric friends swore their allegiance to just such a group, Rote Abend, or Red Evening.

What the members of Rote Abend lacked in experience, they more than made up for with their savage acts of cruelty, inflicted upon the innocent and helpless. A family of four, including two girls under five years old, were killed when the luggage compartment of the bus they were riding in suddenly exploded. A man and his fiancée perished in agony after drinking a bottle of wine into which cyanide had been injected. An automobile manufacturer was gunned down on the steps of his home before the eyes of his horrified wife. The decapitated remains of a pilot in the federal air force were discovered in a ditch. In each instance, Rote Abend had proudly claimed responsibility for the brutal crimes.

Now the BfV and the BND had one of the Red-Evening devils in their sights. Capturing Heisler and squeezing him for information would reestablish a valuable link to Rote-Abend activities that had been lost a year earlier when a BfV undercover man had been identified by the terrorist group and killed. Heisler's arrest could help break the back of the Rote-Abend monster once and for all.

"How far off this road is the farmhouse?" the BND man questioned.

Ruhl shrugged. "Less than a kilometer, if that."

"Good," the BND man remarked. "Pull to the side of the road and park. We'll make the rest of the journey on foot."

"In this weather?" Fleisch protested. "You must be crazy. We'll be soaked to the skin before we've gone ten steps. I say we drive the car at least halfway up the road to the farmhouse. Ruhl can drive without headlights. He's done it before."

"And what happens if some of Heisler's Red-Evening scum turn onto the road behind us?" the BND man asked. "They'll see our car and know something's up. No, I hate to pull rank, but we'll do as I say.'' He tapped Ruhl on the shoulder with his finger. ''This will do nicely. We'll walk from here.''

Ruhl opened his mouth to object, then closed it again. The sooner he and Fleisch got rid of this BND pain in the ass the better, and the only way they were going to do that was to follow his orders and go for a walk in the rain.

''Whatever you say,'' Ruhl agreed as Fleisch groaned. ''You want us to walk, we'll walk.''

Ruhl steered the Audi to the shoulder of the deserted highway and parked. He killed the engine, and the windshield wipers froze in place. A second later the car's headlights winked out to the tune of raindrops beating upon the roof.

Ruhl unbuckled his seat belt and swiveled around to regard his BND passenger. ''There. Satisfied?''

''Yes. Thank you.''

''Fine.'' The sarcasm in Ruhl's tone belied his words. ''Any more requests before we begin our hike?''

''One,'' the BND man said. ''Raise the hood of the car so it will look as though it's broken down. It will help keep passersby from getting suspicious.''

''Right,'' Ruhl said as he pulled back the hood release. ''Is that it?''

''For now.''

The BND man opened the door and stepped out into the pouring rain. Ruhl and Fleisch quickly followed his example. Ruhl raised the Audi's hood, then the three men set out on foot.

In less than a minute they reached the road Gunther Heisler had turned down. It was paved but only wide enough for one vehicle, and fir trees grew on either side.

The night was cold as well as wet, and no moon or stars shone through the clumps of dark clouds overhead. Brisk gusts of wind rattled the branches of the trees and blew in sheets at the men. They were glad of their ankle-length raincoats.

In single file they trudged down the black ribbon of road to where they had left the Audi on the highway. Soon they left the road to make their way through the trees so as not to be seen by anyone entering or leaving the farmhouse.

Ruhl, in the lead, caught his foot on an exposed root and almost fell, resisting with difficulty the urge to swear out loud. He knew better than to make unnecessary noise this close to a suspected terrorist base of operations.

Each man was armed with his weapon of choice. Ruhl and Fleisch carried Walther PPK 7.62 mm pistols and Heckler and Koch MP-5 submachine guns. Their BND counterpart was also equipped with an H&K subgun, as well as a Walther P-5 9 mm automatic, which he wore in shoulder leather.

Wary of the possible guards posted along their route, the three West-German federal security agents made cautious yet steady progress toward their goal. Fifteen minutes after they'd left the warm dry comfort of their Audi, Ruhl lifted his hand to signal that the farmhouse was directly ahead.

Heisler's Volkswagen van was the only vehicle parked in front of the two-story building, although a barn to the right of the house might have sheltered more cars. Except for a light in an upstairs room, the house was dark.

"Heisler's VW and that's the lot," Fleisch observed in a whisper. "He could be alone in the farmhouse."

"Unless he came here to meet someone who's already here," Ruhl suggested quietly. "Although, if that's true, there should be at least one more car."

"We can't be certain there isn't," the man from the BND stated. "Not until we've had a look in the barn."

They approached the barn from the side so as not to be seen by anyone who might be stationed inside. The ground was muddy, and puddles were everywhere. The going was slow because it would be so easy to slip and fall. One man moved while the other two stood ready to supply cover fire if needed. They made it to the barn without incident.

The barn was damp and drafty and smelled of moldy straw and manure. A thorough inspection revealed no vehicles or personnel.

"So now we know," Fleisch announced. "The odds are that Gunther Heisler is waiting for us in the farmhouse all alone. How do we want to work this?"

The BND agent stepped to the barn door and looked out. Directly opposite where he stood was a door into the farmhouse. The light in the room upstairs where Heisler was believed to be could not be seen, and the entire house appeared to be dark now. He reached his decision.

"Through there." He pointed with the business end of his MP-5. "The back door. Hopefully it will be unlocked. If not, we'll force it. Either way, it's safer than going to the front door and ringing the bell."

Back into the pouring rain went the three men, one at a time crossing from the barn to the back door of the farmhouse. Ruhl turned the knob, and noiselessly the door swung open, allowing the men to enter. Fleisch entered last and locked the door behind him.

The shadowed area they were in seemed to be a combination kitchen and dining room. There was a sink, a refrigerator, an oven and stove, and a table surrounded by six chairs. The white globe of an overhead light dangled above the table like a glass moon. Silently the men removed their raincoats and deposited them on chairs.

Through a doorway they entered a dark corridor. Music drifted from the end of the hall, an instrumental version of a hit tune.

As they started toward the source of the music, the song stopped playing. They could hear a faint voice, a commercial for a headache remedy. Heisler was listening to a radio program.

Music began again and the three men moved quietly down the hall, ever on the alert for danger. The corridor ended in a living room meagerly furnished with a sofa, one end table and an upright lamp, arranged so as to face a fireplace. Doors to other parts of the farmhouse framed the fireplace on either side of the hearth.

A staircase rose from one end of the living room, apparently leading upstairs to where Heisler was listening to the radio. Before they could climb to the second floor, however, they had to make sure that the rooms beyond the fireplace were empty.

The man whom Ruhl and Fleisch privately referred to as Captain BND motioned the pair in the direction of the two doors. They nodded their understanding and headed across the room, Ruhl going to the left of the sofa, Fleisch to the right. The excitement of the moment was evident in the way they moved. Gunther Heisler was upstairs, and he was as good as theirs.

Suddenly the doors bordering the fireplace opened with a crash. High-powered spotlights bathed the room. Ruhl and Fleisch staggered, blinded by the glare. A millisecond later the doomed pair were shredded by a storm of bullets from beyond the open doorways.

The BND agent threw himself to the floor. When the shooting finally stopped he knew both BfV men were dead.

"Throw away your weapons," a man's voice called down to him from the top of the stairs. "Your friends are history and you will be, too, if you do not obey my commands. Believe me, if we had wanted you to join them, it would have been simple to arrange. Throw away your weapons now, or you are a dead man."

The BND operative's mind raced, trying to think of a way out of his predicament. He had no options. Anything but surrendering his weapons would find him sharing the fate of Ruhl and Fleisch. The fact that he had not been killed along with them told him there was more to the ambush than met the eye. Rote Abend obviously had plans for him.

"All right." The BND man slowly sat up. "I will do as you say." With the spotlights still shining in his face, he could not see any of his Rote-Abend foes.

"I am carrying a machine pistol and a Walther automatic," he went on, gently removing the MP-5's nylon lanyard from his shoulder, then tossing the gun, stock first, toward the sofa and the lights. He cautiously removed the Walther P-5 9 mm automatic from his shoulder holster and sent it after the MP-5.

"There's a good boy," Gunther Heisler said as he started down the stairs. "I knew we could depend upon you."

Heisler spoke to someone near the fireplace. "Get rid of that garbage there. And see that their Audi disappears." Then he was at the bottom of the steps and staring the BND man in the face.

"What kept you so long? We were beginning to think you and your late friends had decided not to try to capture me tonight, after all. I'm so pleased to see that your sense of duty prevailed. The question is... now that we have you, what are we going to do with you? By the way, I know we've just met, but I do want us to be friends. Would you mind if I simply called you Karl? Herr Hahn seems much too formal."

Karl Hahn showed no reaction to Heisler's knowing his name. He replied, "Karl will be fine... Gunther."

2

"Come see me. We need to talk."

It was an offer Hal Brognola could not refuse, not when it came from the President of the United States. As he sat waiting to be ushered into the Oval Office, the country's top federal agent could only guess why he had been summoned to Washington, but he had little doubt that the executive order had something to do with the men under his command.

Hal Brognola was in charge of Stony Man, the ultrasecret organization formed to fight on behalf of the free world against the rising tide of international terrorism. Two tough antiterrorist squads, Phoenix Force and Able Team, waged this new war on many fronts throughout the world. Hal Brognola was fiercely proud of these valiant warriors.

"The President will see you now," the presidential aide said to Brognola.

"Thank you," Brognola responded. The aide ushered him into the Oval Office to a plush chair opposite the President's desk, then turned without comment and left.

The President looked weary, angry and very much alone. "Thanks for coming on such short notice, Hal," he said when the aide had closed the office door. "Sorry for the inconvenience, but this matter was not one I could discuss over the phone."

"Whatever you say, sir."

The President paused and pushed a humidor across the desk. "Be my guest."

The head fed selected a cigar, which he did not light but clamped between his teeth. "Thank you, sir," he said. "I'm listening."

"Very well, then." The President paused again, and Brognola wondered why he seemed so reluctant to get on with his story. "There's no easy way to tell you this, Hal."

"No need to sugarcoat anything on my account. Am I here because of something concerning Stony Man?"

"Yes and no," the President replied. "When I've explained the situation, you'll understand what I mean. It's like this. Earlier today I received word from our European intelligence sources that two West-German BfV agents had been found murdered. Credit for the deed is being claimed by a particularly evil terrorist group called Rote Abend. In English that means Red Evening."

"I am familiar with the group, sir. For the past year or so Rote Abend has been making quite a name for itself with murder and mayhem."

"Yes, well, tragic though the deaths of the two BfV men may be, that's not why I've asked you here this afternoon. There is, unfortunately, another reason."

"I suspected as much," Brognola said.

"Apparently the BfV pair who were killed were working on the Rote-Abend case with a third man, a member of the Federal Republic of Germany's BND."

At mention of the BND Brognola's jaw clenched, mangling his cigar. "And I know this BND agent personally?" he asked, guessing what the answer would be.

"I'm afraid so. His name is Karl Hahn. Hahn was taken prisoner by Rote Abend at the time the BfV men were killed."

"And where is Karl now?"

"To be honest, we're not sure."

Shocked by the news, Brognola stifled the expletive that sprang to his lips, and sighed instead. Although not a permanent member of the Stony Man team, Karl Hahn had worked with Phoenix Force on several occasions, most of them while Rafael Encizo was sidelined with injuries, and had distinguished himself on the battlefield. Now he had been captured by the very jackals he had dedicated his life to destroying. The thought of Hahn trapped in a web of evil and corruption made Brognola feel sick.

"If Rote Abend has Hahn and they haven't killed him, what do they intend to do with him? Do we know that?"

The President nodded. "We do. Rote Abend wants to trade Hahn for Josef Roetz, a West-German spy who funneled classified information into East Germany for more than thirty years. They've offered to set Hahn free, if the authorities in West Germany do the same with Roetz."

"So what's the problem?" Brognola asked. "They nabbed Roetz once. They can do it again. The important thing is to save Hahn's life. It's no secret how these terrorist packs operate. If Roetz is not delivered to Rote Abend, then Hahn's a dead man."

"I agree wholeheartedly," the President confessed. "And, if it was within their power, I'm sure the West Germans would not hesitate for a moment to make the proposed trade."

"Then what's preventing them?"

"Josef Roetz is dead, committed suicide in his cell in Stuttgart's Stammheim Prison earlier this week. Only a handful of people know about the suicide, and steps have been taken so that the news doesn't get out until this business with Hahn is cleared up."

"Shit!" Brognola muttered. "It sounds as though it will take a miracle."

"Not necessarily. I have it on the strictest authority that the West-German government is doing everything within its power to secure Mr. Hahn's release."

"Which is pretty pointless," Brognola said, "unless Roetz happened to have a twin brother. Am I to assume, sir, that Hahn's predicament means a mission for Phoenix Force?"

The President leaned forward. "No, Hal," he replied earnestly. "I'm sorry. I'm afraid this is one mission Phoenix Force will have to observe from the sidelines. You can see now why I preferred to discuss this business with you face to face."

Brognola chose his words carefully while he took a deep breath and let out the air slowly. "You're telling me, sir, that Stony Man is to abandon Hahn, then?"

"Hahn is a citizen of West Germany, and as I said, the West Germans will do everything they can to save his life."

"And if they fail, Mr. President?"

"We're hoping they don't."

"Yes, but if they do fail," Brognola said, "keeping Phoenix Force out of the action may be denying Karl Hahn his only chance for survival."

"Even if Phoenix Force did have the green light on this, we don't know they could handle the situation any better than the West Germans."

"Granted," Brognola concurred, "but based upon their successful missions to date, you must admit that Phoenix Force would have a damn good chance to pull it off. After what Hahn has done for us, I would think we owed him that much at the very least."

"I understand how you feel, Hal, and I sympathize, but there are other factors at work here that must be taken into consideration."

"Such as?" Brognola asked, unable to completely bottle up his anger. "What's more important than saving a friend's life?"

"It's not as easy as that."

"You're asking me to tell my men that Hahn's out in the cold and they have to leave him there. They'll damn well want to know why."

"Very well, then. I expect you're right. Phoenix Force must not intervene on Hahn's behalf at this time because their interference could undermine the strength of our European defense.

"Times have changed, Hal. Twenty years ago you would have been hard-pressed to find one West-German citizen who didn't view the Soviet Union as the primary source of tension in Europe. Since then, however, such a hard-line stance has become a rarity. The Soviets are still looked upon as villains, but now another country shares the spotlight with them."

"Namely, the United States."

"Exactly. A few years ago the West-German elections saw the emergence of a popular political slogan. Everything had to be 'in the German interest.' If something wasn't for the good of Germany as a whole—and here I'm talking West and East Germany both—then the public didn't want to know about it.

"The general elections that have just concluded illustrate how the political tide has turned against us more than ever. Today many West Germans look back nostalgically to the good old days, to a time when their cultural values were intact and their country was untainted by foreign influence.

"They feel they're pawns in the East-West conflict, and they're fed up with it, want to put a stop to it once and for all. And the way to do that, many feel, is to withdraw West-German support for the U.S. Strategic Defense Initiative and to remove all U.S. nuclear missiles from the area."

"Which would serve as an invitation to the Soviets," Brognola said, "that the rest of Europe was up for grabs."

"The West Germans, especially those belonging to the Social Democratic Party, see things differently. They see the Soviet Union more as a partner than a foe."

"To watch that partnership at work, the SDP should take a long hard look at Afghanistan."

"I know, Hal," the President confessed sadly. "I don't like it any more than you do, but it's the kind of narrow-minded thinking we're up against. The SDP believes that improvement of relations with the Soviet Union and Eastern Europe is the only way to achieve a secure partnership between all parties."

"The same kind of partnership Finland enjoys," Brognola felt obliged to mention. "Finnish foreign policy dictates that they do nothing to disturb the Soviets, and in return the Soviets guarantee Finnish sovereignty by promising not to invade their country.'' The head fed frowned. "Brilliant!" ·

"We can't always make the rules, but we still have to play by them," the President continued. "And right now the rules say that we have to keep a low profile.

"The American presence in West Germany is balancing on a high wire, and it wouldn't take much to cause us to fall. Quite honestly, if that happens, it's the beginning of the end. Country by country, Western Europe will be drawn into the sphere of Soviet influence.

"Too many West Germans are looking for any excuse they can find to justify shooting us down, and I don't want to give them one. Sending Phoenix Force in to rescue Karl Hahn might not automatically knock us off the high wire, but I can't risk it. We have too much at stake. It may be difficult for the men of Phoenix Force to accept, but I would hope they could understand what I'm up against."

"Even at the expense of sacrificing Karl Hahn to the Rote-Abend wolves?"

"*Especially* if it means sacrificing Hahn. It's important that you convey my feelings to your men. They must be made to understand that my decision not to send them to Mr. Hahn's aid was not made easily. I'm depending upon you to relay my message to Phoenix Force just as I've told it to you."

Brognola took the battered cigar from his mouth and said, "You have my word on that, Mr. President." Then he added, "Tell me, sir?"

"Yes, Hal?"

"It's now Thursday evening in Bonn. How long have Rote Abend given the West Germans to come up with Roetz, before they go ahead and execute Hahn?"

"They have until dawn Monday," the President answered. "Three days."

Brognola pushed back his chair and stood. "I see. Well, if you'll excuse me?"

"Of course."

3

The atmosphere inside the War Room at Stony-Man headquarters was fraught with anger and disbelief. Hal Brognola had expected Phoenix Force to be dissatisfied with the President's hard-line stance on Karl Hahn's situation, and he had been proved correct. To a man, the Phoenix-Force warriors vehemently disagreed with the President's decision, and they were forthright in voicing their objections.

"Shit!" David McCarter protested, stubbing out his Player's cigarette furiously. "What a load of rubbish! The day hasn't dawned when I'll sit idly by while a mate of mine gets a lot of stick."

McCarter had come by his strong sense of loyalty growing up in London's tough East End, where your mate was your mate and that was that. An antiterrorist of the highest caliber, McCarter was a veteran of Great Britain's Special Air Service and a former national champion for the British marksmanship team. Before signing on with Phoenix Force, the fox-faced Briton had seen action in Southeast Asia, Hong

Kong and Oman and had participated in the celebrated SAS assault on the Iranian Embassy in London.

"If Hahn is in trouble," McCarter went on impatiently, "then it's up to us to do everything in our power to help him out."

The tall, lanky black man sitting across from McCarter said, "David's right, Hal. It goes against the grain for us to sit tight when Hahn's likely to be put on ice. Karl's saved my ass more than once. I owe him."

"I understand your feelings, Calvin," Brognola replied, "but it's not that simple."

"Neither is letting a friend of mine go down the tubes without a fight," Calvin James growled. "Hell, that's why we're on this hayride, isn't it? To keep trash like Rote Abend from getting away with murder."

The medic of Phoenix Force, Calvin James started life in Chicago's South Side, and later trained in the Navy as a hospital corpsman. In Vietnam he served with the elite SEALS, then came home to study medicine and chemistry under the GI Bill. After his mother and sister died as victims of drug pushers and muggers, he joined the San Francisco Police Department and eventually became a member of the Special Weapons and Tactics team.

James was invited to join Phoenix Force when one of the original members, Keio Ohara, died in combat.

"What I'm saying," James continued, "is that if the tables were turned and it was any one of us with his ass on the line, you can damn well bet Hahn wouldn't think twice about what to do."

"Of course not," Gary Manning agreed emphatically. "We all know Hahn would risk his life to save ours. I say to hell with excuses. Our place right now is in Bonn."

One of the world's top demolitions experts, Gary Manning was the Phoenix crew's best sniper. The Canadian soldier spent two years in Vietnam as a special observer with the 5th Special Forces. Later he joined the Royal Canadian Mounted Police, entered their counterterrorist division, and was subsequently loaned to West Germany's elite GSG-9 antiterrorist squad.

When the RCMP withdrew from espionage, Manning turned down a desk job and returned to civilian life. He was acting as a security consultant for North American International when he was asked to join Phoenix Force.

"We all know how groups like Rote Abend behave when they don't get what they want," Manning went on, directing his comment to Brognola. "They kill the first thing they can get their grimy hands on, and in this case that happens to be Karl. We could make a difference in how this mess turns out."

"You can say that again," Rafael Encizo said. "I know that I haven't worked with Hahn as often as the rest of you guys, but I'd say he's too damn good a man to throw to the wolves.

"Karl stepped in to pick up the slack while I was gathering dust recovering from my head wound. He was there when we needed him. We all know the risks in this line of work. It's highly likely we would have to turn to Karl again sometime to save our bacon. And how are we going to do that if we sit on our cans now and let him die?"

Rafael Encizo had lost his parents and elder brother to Castro's execution squads, and his two sisters and one brother, Raul, to Marxist brainwashing centers. Taken prisoner in the failed Bay of Pigs invasion, he was starved and beaten in El Principe Prison, the hellhole reserved for Castro's political foes. Through a combination of good luck and his own intrepid courage, Encizo escaped to the United States. When singled out to join Phoenix Force, he was employed as an insurance investigator specializing in maritime claims.

Now he shook his head as he reflected on what the President had said to Brognola. "The President wants us to watch this show from the bleachers, because if we intervene on Hahn's behalf it could jeopardize the U.S. presence in West Germany.

"I'm sure the President is sincere about wanting to maintain a low profile, but the logic of such a move escapes me. When the rest of the world sees that the United States has gone soft on its West-German interests, that's when East Germany will start extending the boundaries of its front yard to include all of Europe.''

Yakov Katzenelenbogen nodded in agreement. ''Rafael is correct. If history has taught us anything it's that wearing blinders and pretending a problem doesn't exist in the hope that it will disappear simply does not work. Ignorance may be bliss, but sooner or later that ignorance is paid for with the blood of innocents.''

To the casual observer Yakov Katzenelenbogen could have passed for a middle-aged shoe salesman whose sole source of excitement revolved around the latest style in seasonal footwear. The Israeli colonel's slight paunch, close-cropped, iron-gray hair and gentle blue eyes did nothing to alter this impression. But appearances are deceiving.

Katzenelenbogen was the unit commander of Phoenix Force, a position he enriched with a wealth of personal experience. While a teenager, he had battled alongside the Resistance fighters in Europe against the Nazis. At the close of the Second World War he had joined the Haganah and battled for Israel's independence, and afterward worked with the Mossad. Katz had lost his right arm during the Six Day War, the same grueling conflict that had claimed the life of his only son.

''Let's put aside for a moment the fact that Rote Abend has Hahn—'' Katz gestured with his three-hooked prosthesis ''—and concentrate instead on the fact that they're willing to trade Karl's life for that of Josef Roetz, a man who spent the past thirty years spying for the Communists in East Berlin. That tells us right there that there's more to this than just another bunch of crazies out to change the world. It tells us where Rote Abend's seed money probably originates.''

''True,'' Brognola said, munching on a cigar, ''but that in itself is nothing new. Since the late sixties it's been suspected that many terrorist organizations collect paychecks printed in the red ink of Mother Russia. The possibility that they're on the Communists' payroll doesn't make Rote Abend unique.''

''Of course not,'' Katz concurred, ''but it convinces me that the sooner Rote Abend is put out of action the better. The Communists aren't into charity. They don't shell out money where they won't make a decent return on their investment. My gut instinct tells me that there is more to Rote Abend's schedule of upcoming events than merely kidnapping Hahn and trading him for Roetz.

''Without investigating further we can't second-guess what that 'something' is, but if the Reds are footing the bill, then what Rote Abend has on tap is damn well going to be nasty. Saving Karl's life is important, but so is stopping Rote Abend. It's a conclusion I would make even if Hahn's life weren't at stake.''

Brognola shrugged, wishing he were anywhere else on the face of the earth. "I can only repeat what I've already told Calvin. I understand how you feel. Hell, I feel the same way! But what can I do? I take my orders from the President, and the President says that, as far as Karl Hahn and Rote Abend are concerned, Phoenix Force is not to get involved. I'm sorry. I don't like it any more than you, but my hands are tied."

McCarter scraped back his chair and jumped to his feet. "Well, *my* hands aren't tied."

"What's that supposed to mean, David?" Brognola asked, raising his eyebrows in a worried frown.

"Just what it sounds like," the Cockney said. "I don't need this aggravation. If the President won't let us go to Bonn as a team, then I'll bloody well go there on my own. If the President won't let us try and save Karl, then that cuts it. I'm packing it in."

"What do you mean?" Brognola asked sharply. "You're quitting Phoenix Force?"

McCarter shook his head. "Let's just say that until the problem with Karl Hahn is settled, I'm on strike. The President should be able to accept that, coming from me. In Old Blighty, going on strike is a national pastime."

"I'm not sure that the President will see it that way," Brognola said, inwardly proud of the Englishman's sense of commitment, but unable to voice his approval. "He could very well take this strike as your formal resignation."

"Hard cheese if he does." McCarter's resolve was firm. "My mind is made up."

Gary Manning pushed away from the conference-room table and stood, also. "I'm about due for a vacation myself, Hal. If the President asks, you can tell him I'm in Germany looking up an old friend I haven't seen for a while."

Now Rafael Encizo was on his feet. "And I think I'll go with Gary. During my last visit to Germany, I spent most of my time inside a U.S. military hospital. I think I'd like to get out and rub elbows with the natives, maybe drink a little beer, eat a little schnitzel, take in the sights and make like a tourist."

Brognola looked over to where James was already standing. "How about you, Calvin? Don't tell me you foresee a trip to Germany in the near future."

"You never can tell," James said. "You know, I really love classical music." He glanced to the rest of his teammates. "Does anybody know where Beethoven was born?"

"I think it was in Bonn," Manning offered.

James smiled. "I hope you're right. I'd hate to make the trip for nothing."

Brognola turned to Katz. "And where do I forward your mail for the next couple of days?"

"Keep it for me," Katz said. "I doubt I'll have the time to read it, anyway."

4

The fact that he had not been beaten or tortured by his captors was not altogether comforting to Karl Hahn. Such physical abuse, he knew, would make him damaged merchandise, and for some reason Gunther Heisler and his Rote-Abend crazies wanted him alive and in one piece. So far so good, but Hahn wondered how long he would stay that way.

At the farmhouse where Ruhl and Fleisch had lost their lives and he had been captured, Hahn had been blindfolded, bound and gagged and stuffed into the trunk of the car. He had not been drugged for the journey, so he had been able to judge that the trip took less than one hour and to conclude from that that he was still somewhere in the vicinity of Bonn.

Hahn had then been led from the car to the windowless rooms he had called home for the past two days; there his blindfold had been removed.

One room was furnished with a mattress on the floor and a single woolen blanket, no pillow. The second room adjoined the first. It was scarcely larger than a closet, and held a toilet and sink. A paper cup and a dingy faded towel were provided there.

The walls of both rooms were formed from rough-hewn stone blocks that were cold to the touch. That fact, coupled with his having had to stumble down some steps when he arrived, convinced Hahn that he was being held prisoner in a basement.

Lighting in the rooms came from bare light bulbs dangling from the ceiling, one in each room. The lights stayed on as long as Karl stood or sat on the wire grillwork that covered the entire floor. When he lay or sat on the mattress the lights went out.

Directly above the mattress an air duct protected by a metal screen kept both rooms ventilated and reasonably warm. Another metal screen not far from the first covered a speaker.

The focal point in the larger room was a full-length mirror set into the wall opposite the mattress. Each time he looked at the mirror Hahn had to resist the urge to wave.

Hahn sat on the mattress with his back against the wall, patiently waiting in the pitch-black room. It was almost time to eat. Armed guards brought him bland but satisfying meals three times a day, a practice that negated whatever Rote Abend had hoped to gain by confiscating his watch. He had eaten five times since his capture, and unless he was wrong, tonight's supper was already on the stove.

Too many unanswered questions troubled the methodical Hahn, not the least of which was how Gunther Heisler had known his name. Equally puzzling was why his life had been spared. Were Heisler and his friends holding him for ransom, or did they have something more sinister tucked up their murdering sleeves?

Suddenly the lights came on without his having stepped on the floor. Give or take an hour or so, it had to be close to six o'clock in the evening. Dinnertime.

The solid steel door of his cell opened and four men entered. Hahn had seen three of the four previously—a pair of mute gunmen who kept their H&K MP-5 9 mm machine pistols trained on Hahn and gave the impression they would like nothing better than to cut him down on the spot, and a third terrorist, who now handed Hahn a plate of boiled cabbage and roast beef.

Hahn accepted the food, then watched as the fourth man, who was unarmed, motioned for the other three to leave. This they did in a matter of seconds, leaving the door open just a crack behind them. Hahn felt he should know the name of the fourth man, but it eluded him.

"Your needs are well seen to?" the man inquired. He appeared to be in his late fifties, was of average height and weight and spoke in heavily accented German. "You are treated well?"

"Who wants to know?" Hahn countered.

"My name is Gregor Churatov," the man replied.

"Hmm." Hahn was unimpressed. "You'll forgive me if I don't speak to you in your native tongue, but my Russian is a little rusty."

"It is not the easiest language to learn," Churatov said. "Turkish is out of the question, but we could speak English if you wish."

"German is fine. 'When in Rome' and all that."

"Very well." Churatov showed his teeth in a blatantly phony smile. "No doubt you have questions running through your mind?"

"No doubt I do, but I figure you'll tell me what you want me to know when you're good and ready."

"That is correct," Churatov said. "But before I do that, let me save us both a lot of time by telling what I know of you."

Hahn tasted his cabbage and found it too salty. "I'm listening."

"Good." Churatov took a deep breath and then launched into a series of facts about his prisoner. "You are Karl Hahn, an agent with the BND, and you were formerly with your country's counterterrorist team, the GSG-9. You were transferred to the BND after you personally tracked down and murdered several members of the German Red Army. I believe you claimed your victims had killed a close friend of yours."

"No," Hahn corrected. "When I found my friend he had been tortured and castrated, and had had his eyes gouged out. I'm the one who put what was left of him out of his misery... with a bullet to the brain.''

"And then began your vendetta.''

"They were all 'just executions,'" Hahn stated. "The Red Army monsters were killed swiftly and without mercy, but not one of them had to suffer a fraction of what my friend endured.''

"That is your version of the story,'' Churatov said. "But as we both know, every coin has two sides.''

"And every lie contains a grain of truth. The Red-Army faction members got nothing more than they deserved.''

Churatov continued. "You are fluent in German, English and Turkish, speak Czech and French passably and have, thank you, a smattering of Russian. You attended high school in Southern California, after which you studied computer programming at UCLA. You are skilled in all phases of electronics, and are rated something of a weapons expert.''

Hahn paused over his food. "Someone has done his homework. Is there anything else?''

"Some. For more than eight years you were stationed in Istanbul, and you may or may not have been involved in the disruption of a Soviet business venture there a few years ago.''

Hahn deadpanned it, neither confirming nor denying Churatov's suspicions.

"After Turkey,'' Churatov went on, "you returned to West Germany and worked on a variety of BND assignments. For several months last year you dropped out of sight completely. One report speculated that you had traveled to the United States for a vacation, but we cannot say for certain. Quite frankly, that is the only blank spot we have on you.''

Hahn was relieved to hear this news, because the ''blank spot'' Churatov referred to was the period he had spent as a temporary member of Phoenix Force. Churatov's ignorance of Hahn's involvement with the Stony-Man supersquad did not surprise him, however. Not even Hahn's friends or his close associates in the BND had an inkling of what he had been up to during his extended leave of absence the previous year.

''Congratulations on gaining access to my file,'' Hahn said when he saw that Churatov was finished. ''I won't ask how much it cost you to obtain it.''

''And I wouldn't tell you if you did ask,'' Churatov said. ''Let me assure you, though, that we consider it money well spent. Familiarizing ourselves with your personal history convinced us that you were the man we were looking for. You are an excellent agent, Herr Hahn, and we are betting that the BND will not wish to lose you.''

''If you are expecting the BND to hand over a fantastic sum of money for my safe return,'' Hahn said, ''then I am afraid you and Gunther Heisler and the rest are setting yourselves up for a major disappointment. The BND will not negotiate with terrorists to purchase my freedom with deutsche marks.''

Churatov flashed his phony smile again. "I don't recall saying we initiated your capture for economic gain. Not at all. We have no intention of letting your government off so easily. Rote Abend needs no additional funding, not when it can get all the money it wants from us.

"And because I suspect you are too proud or too stubborn to inquire, I will tell you straight out what we expect the Federal Republic of Germany to pay for your release. What we are proposing is a prisoner exchange. We will trade you to them for someone we would like to have back on our side of the fence. Cut and dried. It could not be more simple."

"And am I supposed to know this prisoner you plan on trading for me?"

Churatov nodded. "I believe so. His name is Josef Roetz."

"Oh?" Hahn remarked, hoping Churatov would not notice his sharp intake of breath. "Josef Roetz, the spy being held in Stammheim Prison." Hahn ate the last morsel of food on his plate. "An interesting choice, this Roetz. There are those who believe that if he tells all he knows about his activities over the past thirty years, his disclosures could prove most embarrassing for the Soviet Union."

"If at all possible—" Churatov shrugged "—we would rather not see that happen, of course. And that is where you enter the picture, Herr Hahn. By exchanging you for Josef Roetz, we fully expect to avoid any such unpleasant publicity."

"But only if my government agrees to trade me for Roetz," Hahn said quickly, "which I seriously doubt they will do."

"If you are right, then that is unfortunate for both of you," the Russian said. "But in the long run it is more unfortunate for you. Unless your government gives us Josef Roetz, I promise you will die."

"When is this proposed exchange to take place?" Hahn asked.

"I see no harm in letting you know," Churatov said. "We have given your government a deadline of dawn on Monday to comply with our demand. If they elect not to do so, well, I have already explained to you the consequences." Churatov held out his hand for Hahn's empty plate. "But enough conversation for now. You have had your supper. I've yet to have mine. We will talk again."

Hahn gave Churatov the plate, then watched the Russian walk from the room. The great steel door was locked as soon as he was gone. Hahn got up from the mattress and went into the next room to get a drink of water, his mind racing at Churatov's revelation.

Josef Roetz! Of all the people they could have picked to trade him for, Rote Abend had to choose a dead man! Hahn was one of the few men in all of West Germany who knew Josef Roetz had committed suicide. Obviously, that secret would have to be revealed in two days' time.

Hahn filled the paper cup with water and carried it to the other room. Rote Abend's demands were, of course, impossible to fulfill, and once the terrorist group and their Soviet backers understood this, the only thing sparing Hahn a miserable death would be gone.

Hahn was confident his government would not abandon him without a fight, but knew the odds were against their finding him before it was too late. And in the meantime what was he to do?

Escape was out of the question. The only way in or out of his cell was through the steel door, but even if he were able to open it and leave, there was certain to be a lead-lined reception committee waiting for him on the other side.

No, with Josef Roetz dead, his only hope for surviving his capture by the Rote Abend killers was for the BND, the BfV or seven GSG-9 to find him. That was the bottom line. Unless... Another possibility occurred to Hahn. Unless somehow Phoenix Force got into the act.

Hahn considered that idea as he finished drinking his water and returned the empty cup to its place on the sink. His friends from Stony Man could make all the difference in the world, assuming, of course, that they were even aware of his situation.

Granted, intervention by Phoenix Force did not automatically guarantee they would accomplish any more than the BND, BfV or GSG-9 could, but Hahn knew that the men of the Force would go to hell and back if they thought doing so might save his life.

Hahn knew Phoenix Force would do this, because he would do the same for any one of them.

5

Without officially sanctioning their unauthorized mission to Germany, Hal Brognola did not intervene to prevent Phoenix Force from catching the next MAC chartered flight from McGuire Air Force Base, New Jersey, to Rhein-Main Air Base near Frankfurt.

Total flying time to Frankfurt was just under eight hours. A special authorization certificate bearing the President's signature—obtained from Stony Man prior to their departure—exempted their luggage from inspection upon their arrival.

Civilian passengers flying to Rhein-Main via MAC transport were usually met by their sponsors and then cleared from there for travel to their ultimate destination in West Germany. The fastest way for Phoenix Force to get to Bonn was to catch a shuttle bus for the ten-minute ride from Rhein-Main Air Base to Frankfurt International Airport.

Due to the heavy volume of weekend traffic out of Frankfurt, the few flights going to Bonn were fully booked. Undaunted, Katz led the way to another

ticket counter. Soon the five were boarding the Lufthansa Airport Express, the only train in the world
owned and operated by an airline.

As the high-speed train left Frankfurt to travel along
the west bank of the Rhine toward Bonn, Phoenix
Force settled back in their private compartment to
collect their thoughts and finalize their plan of action
once they reached Bonn.

A brochure provided for passengers informed them
that the train's top speed was two hundred kilometers
an hour, or roughly one hundred twenty-five miles an
hour, which would put them in Bonn in a fraction of
the time it would have taken to make the journey by
car. When they had been under way for ten minutes,
a Lufthansa stewardess stopped to offer them a meal.
All declined but McCarter, who ordered two cans of
Coke. Once the drinks were delivered Phoenix Force
got down to business.

"When we get to Bonn," Katz began, "we must be
careful not to arouse the attention of the local authorities. We're working under enough time con-
straints here without having the *polizei* to contend
with."

"How long do you think we have before the
President learns what we're up to?" Encizo asked.

"That will depend on what action Hal takes now
that we're out of the country," the Israeli responded.
"He could go for broke and hope the President
doesn't find out, but that isn't Hal's style. It's also not

like him to fence us in when he knows what we're trying to do is right."

"That sort of puts Hal smack dab between a rock and a hard place," James said. "If he tells the President the five of us have gone to Germany, then we could all be on a dozen most-wanted lists by morning."

"Conceivably that could happen," Manning agreed, "if the President decided to reel us in the hard way."

"No," McCarter added, "I think Hal will have to tell the President, but he'll wait until sometime tomorrow to do it. That way we'll have a day's head start, and may even be able to come up with some clue to Hahn's whereabouts. That would make it harder for the President to issue a recall."

"Of course, if past missions are any indication of what's waiting for us in Bonn," Manning said, "then Hal may not have to tell the President anything. The news media may do the job for him."

"Hal and the President would just love that," Encizo commented.

"I tend to go along with David," Katz said. "We should figure on a minimum of twenty-four hours before we get any flak from the White House. Until then, I think we're on our own." Katz glanced at Gary Manning. "How sure are you that this friend of yours from GSG-9 will help us?"

"I think we can count on him," the Canadian answered. "Dieter Beck and I go way back. I haven't seen him since I was here on loan to GSG-9, but we've been in touch off and on. Last I heard Dieter had changed jobs."

"What's he doing now?" Encizo asked.

"Working for the BKA," Manning replied, referring to the *bundeskriminalamt*, West Germany's Federal Criminal Investigation Office. "Normally that would put Dieter in Wiesbaden, where the BKA operates its national headquarters, but they also maintain a major field office in Bonn that provides protection for government officials, along the same lines as the U.S. Secret Service."

"GSG-9 or BKA," Katz said, "it makes no difference to us so long as Herr Beck isn't shy about pitching in on the side."

"If he's still the Dieter I remember, then we have nothing to worry about," Manning promised. "Dieter Beck hates terrorists almost as much as we do."

FRAU BECK ANSWERED the door on the third ring of the bell. Manning, who spoke fluent German, did the talking. First he introduced himself and apologized for dropping by at such a late hour, and then he politely asked to speak to Dieter. Frau Beck told Manning and the others to please wait, then disappeared back inside her house. A minute later she returned with her husband.

Catching a glimpse of Manning, Dieter Beck smiled and stepped out onto his front porch. "When Annette told me there was a Herr Manning asking to see me, you can imagine my surprise."

"Hello, Dieter," Manning said, gripping Beck's hand in a firm handshake. "I hope you hadn't already retired for the evening?"

"What? You must be joking. Since when did the workday ever end because the sun went down? But why are we talking outside like strangers? Please, you and your friends must accept our hospitality. Come."

Dieter Beck and his wife led Manning and the others into their house and down a hallway that opened into a comfortably furnished sitting room. The introductions began as soon as everyone was gathered inside, Beck formally introducing his wife, Annette, and Manning returning the courtesy by presenting his four companions to the Becks, using the cover names they had decided upon earlier.

Frau Beck's offer of coffee was met with enthusiasm, and as she left to prepare it, Dieter Beck invited his visitors to be seated.

"You should have let me know that you were coming," Beck said. "We could have enjoyed a meal together. Annette is a wonderful cook."

Manning grinned. "So I can see."

Beck's smile was just as wide as he patted his rounded stomach. "What can I say in my defense?

Annette loves to cook—I love to eat. It is a marriage made in heaven.''

"Do you mind, Dieter?" Manning asked. "Not all my friends speak German. Would English be all right?"

"Of course." Beck effortlessly switched languages. "You should have mentioned it sooner. So tell me, Gary, how have you been? I know you are no longer with the RCMP. If I remember correctly you work for some big firm whose name escapes me."

"North American International," Manning supplied. "I'm a security consultant for the company. The work's not quite as exciting as what we used to do, but it keeps me busy and out of trouble."

"I'm sorry to hear that," Beck said with a trace of amusement in his voice. "What brings you to Bonn, then? Business or pleasure?"

"I wish it were pleasure, Dieter, but I'm afraid that will have to wait until next time. I came to see you tonight because a good friend of ours is in some very deep trouble, and I am hoping you will be able to help us to help him."

"Then I am glad you did not forget Dieter Beck. If it is help you need and I can provide it, then you shall have it," Beck assured Manning confidently. "This friend of yours who is in trouble...may I know who he is?"

The Canadian commando nodded. "His name is Karl Hahn."

Beck nodded, obviously recognizing the name. "Hmm, Karl Hahn. The fact that you know Hahn's name tells me you haven't entirely given up your ties with the past. Even here in West Germany not many people know what has become of your friend. I am impressed."

Beck paused as his wife brought the coffee. Frau Beck told her husband to call out if they needed anything else, then left the room.

"How much do you know?" Beck asked Manning.

"Basically this. We know Hahn was taken prisoner by Rote-Abend terrorists following a gunfight at a farmhouse outside Bonn. The two BfV agents with Hahn were killed. A prisoner exchange has been proposed for a man who spied for the East Germans for the past thirty years. That spy is Josef Roetz, who until a few days ago, was being held in the maximum security section of Stammheim Prison in Stuttgart. However, Roetz recently committed suicide, allegedly by stabbing himself in the throat with a fork. Roetz's death means that the trade Rote Abend wants cannot take place."

"And if the trade does not take place," Beck said, "then Karl Hahn dies. Now I am really impressed. It is a mystery how you know what happened to Hahn, but I could perhaps puzzle it out given the time. The other, though? Well, let me say that the knowledge of Josef Roetz's suicide automatically puts you and your friends in a very exclusive group. As far as the rest of the world is concerned—and that applies especially to those Rote-Abend bastards—Josef Roetz is still alive. And as long as the rest of the world continues to believe in that lie, then Karl Hahn lives.''

"Or at least he does until dawn Monday when your government fails to deliver Roetz to Rote Abend," Katz suggested.

"Verfluchte!" Beck swore in German, then he said to Manning, "What I am hearing does not say much for the tight lid of security we're supposed to have clamped on this mess."

"Don't feel too bad," Manning consoled his friend. "Our knowledge of the details regarding Hahn's case has nothing to do with a security leak at your end."

"How do you know, then?" Beck asked.

Manning shrugged. "Let's just say we have friends in high places and let it go at that."

"Very high places from the sound of it," Beck commented, "and something tells me that none of them are connected with North American International. Who are you really working for, Gary? It's common knowledge that the CIA uses foreign talent when it suits their purpose, but I would never have pegged you as a so-called Company man."

"Trust me, Dieter," Manning said. "While I am not at liberty to tell you who I or my friends represent, you have my word that we are not with the CIA."

Beck sighed with frustration. "Bah, it wouldn't even matter if you were. All that's important is that you are here to help Hahn, and right now your BND friend is in desperate need of all the help he can get. My earlier promise stands, I will assist you in any way I can. I was not fond of Ruhl and Fleisch, the two BfV who were murdered, but no one deserves to be slaughtered in cold blood as they were. Their Rote-Abend killers must be made to pay for their crimes. And if we can save Hahn's life in the process, so much the better.''

"What can you tell us about local efforts to secure Karl's release?" McCarter asked, sipping his coffee and wishing it were a glass of Coke, instead. "Has a task force been mobilized to handle the situation?"

"Not so you'd know it," Beck admitted. "Official reaction to the incident has been decidedly low-key."

"How low-key?" James wanted to know, clearly not liking the implication of what Beck was saying. "The BND has to be madder than hell that their man got snatched."

"And what about the BfV?" Encizo inquired. "Or your outfit, the BKA? Surely there's some kind of co-ordinated effort to save Hahn's hide?"

"I wish I could say that were true," Beck answered, "but the 'low-key' response I alluded to is precisely that. We have all been ordered to maintain a low profile and hope that established contacts, local informants and the like, will lead us to where Hahn is being held prisoner."

"What?" McCarter suddenly stood up. "That's it? That's *all* that's being done?"

"Our orders are quite explicit," Beck told the Briton.

"Do you have any idea why such instructions were issued?" Katz asked.

"Certainly," Beck said. "It's because of Josef Roetz. Not the fact that Roetz is dead. No, the reluctance to do the job as it should be done stems from those who are really behind the push to release Roetz."

"And by that you mean the Communists," James concluded.

"Exactly," Beck confirmed.

"So what else is new?" Encizo said. "This isn't the first time the Soviet Reds have managed to manipulate events within your country."

"A fact I am well aware of, Herr Brown," Beck said, addressing Encizo by his cover name. "While everyone involved with West German security privately agrees that the Soviet Union bankrolls any number of terrorist activities here and abroad, those directly in charge of policy and, particularly, of dealing with the media will never publicly admit that a link between the Soviets and terrorism even exists. And they can cite reasons for their silence, more than twenty million of them."

"Or roughly the number of Germans living on the eastern side of the Berlin Wall," Katz speculated. "Many of your countrymen don't point the finger of blame where it belongs for fear of disturbing the peaceful coexistence between East and West."

"Yeah," McCarter complained, "well, it's that same peaceful coexistence that's going to get Hahn killed... unless we can pull together and sort out this mess on our own."

Manning asked his friend, "How do you feel about this low profile you've been ordered to maintain?"

The BKA officer thought for a moment, then replied. "Just as you and your friends do, I suspect. Maintaining a low profile because there is danger that the Soviet Union will be offended is a doormat approach to defense. We all know what happens to doormats—they get walked on. If West Germany sticks with this policy long enough, it is inevitable we will get trampled. If there is one thing Moscow finds irresistible, it is an open door and a place to wipe their feet. And when we speak of the Communists' goals, we're not talking simply of muddy feet, but bloody feet, as well."

"That pretty much coincides with our assessment of the situation," Manning said. "The thing is, Dieter, while your assistance will be very helpful to our mission, I don't want you to feel obligated because you and I are friends. We haven't come to Bonn to maintain anything close to a low profile, as far as Rote Abend goes. They are the ones who captured Hahn for the Soviets, and they are the ones who can tell us where to find Karl."

"And if we should happen upon some Rote-Abend garbage," Beck concluded, "they are not likely to surrender any details of Hahn's whereabouts without a fight. This I know.

"Believe me, Gary, I understand the risks. Naturally, for my family's sake, I would not wish any harm to come to me. On the other hand, unless savages like Rote Abend learn that their activities will never be accepted by a free society, then it is our destiny to be forever enslaved by fear. No, you have asked for my help, and that is what you shall have."

Manning smiled. "Thank you, Dieter."

Beck set his coffee cup down and clapped his hands. "So, when do we start?"

"That depends on you," Katz said. "Would to-night be all right?"

"Certainly," Beck agreed. "If you'll give me a minute, I will grab a few things and let Annette know I am going out." He looked at his Canadian friend. "Funny. Until you showed up this evening, Gary, I was looking forward to a typically quiet weekend. Now it seems, we may raise a little hell together."

Manning said, "I'm counting on it, Dieter. We all are."

6

Gary Manning and Dieter Beck knew they had found some Rote-Abend terrorists when, at 2:10 a.m., they passed through the open gate to an abandoned factory site and a bullet from an unseen sniper's rifle drilled a hole through one of the halogen headlights on Beck's Saab 900. Manning and Beck felt the impact of the bullet as the headlight went out in a rush of exploding gas and glass.

"Pay dirt!" Manning reacted, whipping his Desert Eagle .357 from shoulder leather. "We found them!"

"Looks like they found us," Beck observed coolly, throwing the Saab's shift into reverse just as another bullet played hide-and-seek with the car's radiator. "Bastards! They better not total my car. I just paid the damn thing off!"

Glancing over his shoulder, Beck mashed the accelerator to the floor, sending the Saab screeching in reverse. Behind the Saab, in the Volkswagen Quantum sedan Phoenix Force had rented upon arriving in Bonn, David McCarter was backing up hurriedly, too.

Engines raced and rubber burned as the two vehicles retreated to the outside of the wall surrounding the Stern Gerätfabrik.

Unsanctioned though their mission to West Germany was, Phoenix Force had benefited from a hasty briefing on all the facts about Rote Abend that Stony Man's computers could come up with. Hal Brognola had looked the other way when this was going on.

When Phoenix Force sat down with Dieter Beck in Bonn and pooled their information with that of the BKA man, some possible leads emerged to turning up Rote-Abend members, who might in turn reveal where Karl Hahn had been taken.

Phoenix Force had extensive data on Gunther Heisler, including the fact that his current lover among his terrorist followers was a woman called Ilse Stern. Beck reported that the authorities suspected Rote Abend of hoarding arms in derelict warehouses and abandoned factories. He knew that among the properties under suspicion was that of a former appliance manufacturing firm called Stern Gerätfabrik.

It seemed unlikely that Rote Abend would use a site that had once been owned by the uncle of one of its own members. But Phoenix Force and Beck agreed that what was probably just a coincidence should be checked out. To their surprise, the bullets fired at them made it look as if their hunch had paid off.

After their hasty retreat from the factory grounds, the Saab and the Quantum came to a halt within inches of each other. The men inside jumped out.

"You all right?" Katz was quick to ask Manning.

"They hit Dieter's car twice," the Canadian answered. "Anybody get a look at the shooter?"

Katz shook his head. "Too dark." The Israeli colonel was armed with the Uzi submachine gun he favored. His backup piece was a SIG-Sauer P-226 9 mm pistol. "You would know better than us what we should do now," Katz addressed Beck. "Any suggestions?"

Beck, who was holding a H&K MP-5 machine pistol he had used since his days with GSG-9, responded at once. "The factory grounds have two entrances, this one—" he pointed to the open gate nearby "—and another one in back. But the rear entrance was sealed off after the factory shut down last winter."

"That's it, then," McCarter announced, excited. The former SAS commando carried an Ingram MAC-10 SMG draped over his shoulder, and tucked out of sight in a holster beneath his left arm was a Browning Hi-Power 9 mm autoloader. "We're blocking the only way into the place. They have to come out this way or stay put."

"I don't think they plan on staying put." Rafael Encizo, toting like Beck, a H&K MP-5, had run to the edge of the factory's double-wide entry gate. After a further look around the corner of the wall, he withdrew and reported, "There's a whole mob of people piling into a truck. I'm not sure about the rest, but the pair in the cab are both armed."

From the direction of the factory came shouts and the sound of the truck's engine roaring to life. Then the engine revved faster as the vehicle pulled away from the loading bay where it was parked.

"We can't let them past us," Katz said. "We'd better not all be bunched together on one side of the entrance. Spread out."

The truck drew nearer as James responded to Katz's directive. "Let's see if they're paying attention." Crouching low, cradling his S&W M-76 submachine gun, the Phoenix pro from Chicago ran to the edge of the gate, then sprinted across the open space to the wall at the opposite side. Before he reached shelter a stream of hungry bullets began chewing up the ground at his heels. James dived for the clump of weeds that was his goal as the enemy slugs caught up to him, the bullets plowing into the wall above his head.

James scrambled to his feet, and with a note of relief in his voice, called to his companions, "They're paying attention."

"How about you and me giving them something else to think about?" Encizo suggested.

"Sounds like a plan," James returned. "They're about thirty yards away, heading straight for us."

"Got it," the Cuban said.

As the enemy's truck rushed toward them, James and Encizo flew into action, triggering their weapons from opposite sides of the entrance to the factory complex.

The deadly cross fire of Stony-Man lead shattered the advancing truck's windshield in a spray of flying glass that lacerated the driver from his groin to the top of his head. Bleeding from hundreds of cuts, but somehow spared any damage to his eyes, the driver screamed and swerved the truck sharply to the left to avoid taking the canopied flatbed through the hailstorm of death.

The left turn might have made sense to the driver—it placed him on the side of the truck farthest from machine gun fire—but it spelled disaster for the gunman hanging out the open passenger door, who was trying to line up his SMG on the two enemy targets. Thrown off balance by the unexpected change of direction, the killer riding shotgun was just grabbing the top of the door when three 9 mm minirockets from Encizo's MP-5 zapped him in the chest and flung his lifeless body from the speeding truck to the pavement.

His vision impaired now by the blood from a dozen scalp wounds dripping in his eyes, the truck driver had caught only a fleeting glimpse of his passenger's fall from the cab. Then he was forced to slam on the brakes to avoid striking a utility pole that appeared out of nowhere. The truck slowed momentarily, then continued unchecked when the driver's blood-soaked foot slipped from the brake pedal.

What the driver failed to do mechanically, the utility pole accomplished with ease, stopping the truck with a resounding crash that left the pole quivering in its foundation, protruding vertically like a cement breadstick from the front of the truck. Ignoring the screams from his comrades riding in back, the driver slid out of the cab and raced away from the front gate toward the factory building.

The passengers in the rear who had survived the crash poured from the truck like ants from a poisoned anthill, rushing for the factory.

"Come on," James shouted, and he and Encizo charged after their foes. Katz, Manning, McCarter and Beck swiftly followed.

The loading-bay doors leading into the factory building were separated from the front gate by a parking lot and a driveway, a distance of approximately one hundred yards. With the exception of an occasional utility pole that fed electricity to the plant, the area was wide-open territory with no protection from bullets. Two of the men fleeing the twisted wreckage of the truck spun on their heels to open fire on their mysterious attackers, hoping to buy time for the rest of their group to reach the factory safely.

James and Encizo anticipated their move, blasting a path of destruction with their own weapons that quickly enveloped the pair of killers in a curtain of lead-lined doom. Both enemy gunmen fell dead in seconds.

As they ran through the gate, Katz and the others had fanned out, the Israeli colonel and McCarter to the left, Manning and his West-German friend to the right. Manning and Beck stopped for a look at the dead killer who had tumbled from the front seat of the truck before it crashed. His facial features were unmarred.

"Recognize him?" Manning asked.

Beck looked into the dead man's face, then replied, "Klaus Ingberg. Definitely Rote Abend."

"Good," Manning stated, then he and Beck continued their rush.

The truck driver reached the loading-bay doors and kept on going. The pistol clutched in his nervous right hand felt as useless as a hairbrush. Right then the Rote-Abend cause meant nothing to him. Saving his life was all that mattered.

As the driver disappeared inside the abandoned factory a dozen more of the Rote-Abend gang followed immediately in his wake. Once the walls of the building were around them, they felt a small measure of confidence return.

"We can hold them off from here," cried one of the terrorists.

"What in God's name happened?" another demanded. "Peter, Ralf and Karl are dead. Are we to be next?"

"Quiet!" a third Rote-Abend gunman ordered. He was a take-charge brute named Eugen Kremer, who had no intention of sharing the fate of their three dead comrades. "Our attackers are out in the open with no place to hide, where we can pick them off with ease. There will be no more running. I suspect we outnumber our opponents, and even if we don't, it is up to us to balance the odds. They must not be permitted to live."

Kremer pointed to the four Rote-Abend members nearest the loading-bay doors. "Guard the doors well and do not let our enemies through. The rest of us will find a way to circle around and surprise them from behind. To your posts now, and hurry, before it is too late."

The four terrorists on the receiving end of Kremer's orders were not pleased with their role but could appreciate the wisdom of the plan. They obeyed orders and moved into place as Kremer and the seven remaining members of the team hurried farther into the factory. They had scarcely taken their positions near the loading bay, when fresh shots rang through the open doors and the four defenders became three.

Watching one of their own butchered before her eyes prompted a female terrorist named Anita Buch to snarl in anger. "That dirty son of a bitch Kremer's not fooling anyone. He left us to catch the bullets while he and the others save their skins." More slugs sprayed into the factory. "If we stay where we are, we're as good as dead."

"Perhaps not," Heinz Rist said, launching a barrage of hastily aimed subgun fire that hit nothing, but made him feel a little less vulnerable. "The two doors into this loading bay are manually operated."

"So?" asked a slow-witted killer called Manfred. "How does that help us?"

"Idiot!" Anita Buch called as she ran to the chain-and-pulley mechanism nearby. "If we lower the doors, then the murdering bastards cannot get in here. Quick! Lower the door on your side."

"But Kremer said to—"

Manfred's objection was overruled in midsentence by a triple burst of lead from Anita Buch's submachine gun that shaved away the top of his skull in a spurting geyser of gore.

Heinz Rist was already pulling at the release pin for the door on his left as Manfred's body hit the floor. "Was that necessary?"

"Move your ass and ask me later," the female Rote-Abend fanatic ordered. "We may yet get out of this tomb Kremer left us in."

Both release pins were withdrawn and the loading-bay doors began falling into place.

DAVID MCCARTER WAS STILL more than fifty feet away from the rapidly descending doors—too far away to try to get under them before they closed for good, but well within throwing range. In one fluid motion the British commando's hand whipped into his pocket and retrieved an M-33 fragmentation grenade. Pulling the pin with his left hand and holding down the safety lever with his right, McCarter took aim and heaved the ball-shaped bomb at the dwindling space below one of the doors as it dropped into place. His timing was perfect.

The M-33 struck the paved landing of the loading bay and rolled beneath the door a second before it closed. Anita Buch and Heinz Rist recognized the grenade, but it was too late. The explosion tore the flesh from their bones and drained the life from their bodies in a rush of blinding agony.

The preengraved frag did more than end the lives of two Rote-Abend savages. When the M-33's 6.5 ounces of Composition B filler detonated, the loading-bay door ruptured under the tremendous force of the blast, splitting up the middle and creating a hole large enough to serve as a makeshift entrance.

"Looks like our friends left some of their people behind, while the rest vamoosed to higher ground," James said as he and the others joined McCarter. "I caught your act with the grenade. Good pitch."

"I aim to please," said the cockney.

Yakov Katzenelenbogen turned to Manning and Beck. "Do we know for sure whether this gang is Rote Abend?"

"Yes," Manning replied, without letting his attention stray from the hole in the loading-bay door. "Dieter got a positive make on one of the first terrorists we bagged."

"He was definitely Rote Abend," Beck confirmed. "Which means they probably all are. We seem to have stumbled onto something big here."

"One sure way to find out, mate," McCarter announced, breaking away from the others. Holding his Ingram MAC-10 ready to fire, he hurried toward the hole that his M-33 grenade had punched in the door.

As McCarter left the others behind, Dieter Beck turned to Gary Manning and asked, "Is your friend always so eager to tempt death to take him?"

"Don't get alarmed, Dieter," Manning advised, "our British friend is just getting warmed up."

James started after McCarter and added, "Ain't it the truth."

7

"What was that?" a Rote-Abend terrorist questioned as the noise of an explosion reverberated through the factory.

"It sounded like some kind of bomb," another responded. "Coming from the direction of the loading bay."

"Oh, no! You know what that means, then?" the first terrorist insisted fearfully. "Anita and the others must be dead."

Eugen Kremer cut into the conversation to prevent a full-scale case of hysteria. "Just because we heard what may have been a single grenade going off doesn't mean our four friends are lost."

"No?" a skeptic scoffed. "Then why has the shooting stopped? Answer me that!"

Kremer controlled his urge to beat to a pulp those around him who seemed to be showing a cowardly streak. He confronted the seven terrorists who had followed him into the factory and told them exactly what they did not want to hear.

"You're absolutely right," Kremer blurted in a whisper. "Anita and the rest probably *are* dead, and we will all be dead, too, if we don't come to our senses. There's no longer any point in sneaking outside to launch a surprise attack from the rear. Whoever it is we're up against, they are undoubtedly already inside the factory."

"What should we do, then Kremer?" asked a woman carrying an automatic rifle.

Eugen Kremer was relieved that the others were once more looking to him for leadership. "Listen carefully, everyone, so I don't have to tell you twice."

A GRISLY VISTA GREETED David McCarter as he stepped through the twisted hole torn in the loading-bay door. Even in the near darkness of the factory the full extent of the damage caused by the M-33 grenade he had thrown was all too evident on the floor of the loading bay.

On his right lay the headless torso of a Rote-Abend terrorist who was revealed through shredded strips of clothing as female. The dead woman's head had been blasted from her shoulders and had bounced or rolled to a nearby corner. A tangle of hair covered the face.

The Londoner discovered three more bodies on his left, all male, their limbs broken and bent. The ribs of one corpse sprouted through the dead man's chest like a bony picket fence. Another looked as though he had died chewing on his foot.

McCarter turned as Katz and the others silently joined him. There was no reason to speak, especially when the sound of a voice might be all a Rote-Abend sniper needed to zero in on a target.

In its prime the building Dieter Beck had brought Phoenix Force to had been used to manufacture a variety of products, including washers, dryers and microwave ovens. According to Beck, high domestic wages and an influx of inexpensive good-quality imports from the Far East had saturated the marketplace and the factory had finally folded. The gutted shell of the former manufacturing plant was all that remained.

Two passageways large enough for a forklift to travel through branched off from where Phoenix Force and Beck were standing, leading to different parts of the factory complex. Katz motioned for Encizo and McCarter to follow him through one of the passages and directed Manning, James and Beck to take the other. Both parties then continued to search for their adversaries.

Two minutes later McCarter, Katz and Encizo reached the end of the wide corridor and faced an enclosed area the size of a small department store, which had been the actual manufacturing area of the complex. In the darkness little could be seen but shadowy patterns of gray and black. The trio knew any of the obscure pockets of darkness could be serving as hiding places for the enemy.

Encizo slipped his hand into the pocket of his coat and removed a single MK-1 illuminating grenade. Resembling a M-26 fragmentation grenade, the MK-1 was designed to burn at ground level only. It had an illumination charge of twenty-five seconds, and could generate fifty-five thousand candlepower to light an area more than two hundred twenty yards in diameter.

Holding the MK-1 in his right hand, his fingers curled around its safety lever, Encizo withdrew the MK-1's safety pin, then let the grenade fly as far as he could. All three Phoenix Force members shielded their eyes. Seven seconds later the MK-1 flooded the open area with light, revealing eight Rote-Abend terrorists.

The six men and two women had been lying in wait to spring a trap and were caught by the MK-1's fiery glow in a tableau of complete astonishment. Recovering from the shock of discovery, a terrorist who seemed to be in charge shouted for his comrades to fire their weapons. But Phoenix Force got there first.

Partially protected by the walls of the passageway they were standing in, McCarter, Katz and Encizo unleashed the combined firepower of their weapons upon the terrorist trash. First to pay the price for a life of crime and violence was the apparent leader of the band of killers. He was pelted from sternum to crotch by a lead hailstorm from Katzenelenbogen's Uzi. Clusters of dark red blossoms appeared where the bullets hit home, and the doomed terrorist danced and twitched his way into hell.

Temporarily blinded by the stunning explosion of the MK-1 grenade, three fanatics regained their vision just as autofire from Encizo and McCarter stole it away again. One terrorist's life was extinguished when a couple of 9 mm manstoppers bored black holes in his forehead and sent twin spurts of gore mushrooming out the back of his skull.

The next Rote-Abend murderer to perish yawned and tried to scream as a lone bullet plowed through the roof of her mouth. Her arms jerked straight up and her automatic rifle was airborne.

The West-German terrorist beside the dead woman watched a stream of slugs from his submachine gun rip a line of holes across the ceiling; his finger was tightened in a death lock on his subgun's trigger while his body endured repeated hits. Then a burning sensation like a furnace in his chest reached his brain, and nothing else mattered.

Their number reduced by half, the four Rote-Abend terrorists still on their feet lashed out with a series of poorly aimed shots that peppered the wall above and behind where Encizo, Katz and McCarter were holding the fort. Instinctively the Stony-Man trio dropped below the line of fire, then stood again when they saw that the Red-Evening killers had taken advantage of the momentary lapse of counterfire to try to flee through a pair of swinging doors to their left. But their ill-timed escape attempt was futile. The swinging doors slammed open and revealed Manning, James and Dieter Beck, ready to join the battle.

Manning's .357 Magnum cracked twice in the Canadian's hand, lifting the nearest Rote-Abend terrorist off her feet and onto her back for a messy impromptu skid across the floor. The final three enemy gunmen met their fate at the hands of Calvin James and Dieter Beck. Mortally wounded, they collapsed together in a bloody heap, just as the MK-1's charge sputtered and died, and the factory was plunged into darkness once more.

"Good shooting," Katz offered as he and his teammates were reunited.

"Our pleasure," James said. "How many Rote Abend were there altogether?"

"I counted eight," Encizo answered. "Do you—"

"What was that?" Gary Manning turned on his heel and began to run toward the unmistakable sound of breaking glass.

The noise led Manning to a small room that had apparently once served as an office. Its window was broken, the glass kicked or battered from its frame so that only a jagged outline remained.

His boots crunching the shards of glass beneath his feet, Manning crossed to the window to look outside. Cool moist air made him shiver, but he saw nothing.

"What do we have?" McCarter called out as he entered the office.

"One that got away," Manning replied. "No sign of him or her anywhere."

McCarter looked out the window himself. "Maybe we should organize a hunting party."

"No," Katz said as he and the others gathered in the office doorway. "We can't afford to waste the time. Whoever took off through the window isn't going to bother us again for a while, which will give us a chance to find out for sure just what Rote Abend's interest is in this factory. The more we know about the group the better equipped we'll be to defeat them next time. Let's do it."

Splitting into pairs, Phoenix Force and Dieter Beck began a thorough search of the factory. In less than fifteen minutes they found what they were looking for, inside the spacious walk-in freezer of the factory's cafeteria.

"Wonderful," James observed after Encizo and Katz had alerted everyone to their discovery. "These creeps are playing with fire."

Quite literally, they were. In addition to a wealth of incendiary devices such as white phosphorus and Thermite grenades, the freezer also contained a veritable shopping list of weapons for murder and mayhem terrorist-style.

Included among this deadly arsenal were twenty-five machine guns, five hundred pounds of explosives, a dozen antitank grenade launchers with seventy-five grenades, two hundred fifty frag grenades, three hundred bombs and approximately fifteen thousand rounds of ammunition. But the most disquieting item in the freezer was a wide metal cylinder eighteen inches long.

"Isopropanol," Katz read, using a penlight to read the name stenciled along the side of the cylinder. "There's only one thing Rote Abend could use this material for."

"Right," Calvin James agreed, as dread settled over them like a shroud. "Chemical warfare."

8

The terrorist told a tale of disaster the likes of which none of them had ever expected to hear. Rote Abend had been attacked. Beaten. The large cache of weapons hidden at the factory was lost, and everyone there except William Rupp had been killed.

Bleeding from wounds filled with slivers of the broken glass that had sliced seventy-five percent of his body surface, Rupp had dragged himself from the factory to a pay telephone and called Gunther Heisler for help all the while babbling incoherently about an army of commandos descending without warning upon the factory. Heisler had calmed down the hysterical Rupp long enough to determine where he was phoning from, then immediately dispatched two Rote-Abend loyalists to collect the injured man before he could be spotted and picked up by the police.

William Rupp was now stretched out on the clean white sheets of Heisler's bed, slowly but surely bleeding to death, and recounting the details of the inexplicable attack to the more than two dozen Rote-Abend followers crammed into the room.

"Please," Rupp requested faintly.

"Of course," Heisler said, lifting Rupp's head and tilting the glass of whiskey to his trembling lips.

Rupp opened his mouth and swallowed, then allowed Heisler to lower his head gently to the pillow. "It was a miracle I escaped at all. I can still hear the screams of Eugen Kremer and the others. It was horrible. They didn't stand a chance. Our friends were butchered like cattle in a slaughter yard."

"And you have no idea who these men were?" Heisler asked for the tenth time in as many minutes. "GSG-9, perhaps. Or maybe they were BND?"

"There was no way to tell," Rupp insisted. "But I don't think they were either one. The strangers appeared at the factory just after we arrived to empty the freezer of our weapons and supplies. We never even got to the cafeteria. No sooner had we climbed out and made our way into the factory than shots were fired. Someone shouted for me to jump behind the wheel of the truck because we were under attack. The rest I have already told you. Of all who went to the factory tonight, I am the only survivor." Rupp's eyes brimmed over with tears as a fresh wave of pain racked his body.

"These men who attacked the factory," Heisler said, "how many of them were there?"

"Five. Six at the most," Rupp answered, then added, "Please, Heisler."

"More whiskey?" Heisler asked.

"No." Rupp coughed and flecks of blood painted his chin. "The doctor? He will be here soon, won't he?"

"Of course," Heisler lied smoothly. "He will be tending to your needs any minute now. In the meantime, I want you to rest until he arrives. Will you do that for me, Rupp?"

Rupp coughed again and found the strength to nod. "Yes, Heisler. I will rest. But tell the doctor to hurry, will you?"

"Of course," Heisler said. "He will be here before you know it."

Heisler rose from the edge of the bed where he had been sitting and ushered everyone from the room, turning off the bedroom light and closing the door behind him. He led his Rote-Abend comrades downstairs to the meeting room in his converted basement. A fire burned in a fireplace, and there were plenty of chairs for everyone.

Heisler went to a lectern set up in front of the chairs and waited for his comrades to settle before he finally spoke.

"I don't have to impress upon you the severity of the news Rupp brings us," Heisler began. "Never have so many of us fallen at once—and we're not talking about arrest, mind you, but death."

"And yet the evidence speaks for itself," said Ilse Stern, a native of Bonn and Heisler's lover. Compassion burned in her voice. "Rupp is upstairs dying, and we are powerless to help him. He has lost too much blood. Seeking medical attention for him would prove disastrous for us. For all we know the authorities are looking for him even now. And so we must do nothing.

"By morning Rupp will be dead, while those responsible for killing him and so many of our friends will still be roaming free. They have robbed us of the precious weapons and equipment we worked so hard to obtain. We must find out who they are and punish them, or we will all suffer the same fate as those who have died."

"What about the weapons?" a man sitting behind Ilse wanted to know. "How will we ever recover them?"

"Obviously we won't," Heisler told the man, "which is not the tragedy it might seem. That particular cache was only one of many we have hidden throughout the city. Most of what was taken will not be missed. What does concern me, though, is the cylinder of isopropanol we lost. Certainly we have more, but that is not the point. Whoever has the cylinder now will not need a degree from Bonn University to understand why we had isopropanol stockpiled with the rest of our supplies. That knowledge is bound to disturb them."

"Where's the harm in that?" Ilse Stern shrugged. "By the time the fools put two and two together, our reason for obtaining the isopropanol will be history. I say let them lose sleep over what little they know, and forget about it. It's more important to concentrate on repaying our enemies in kind for the deaths of our friends."

"Ilse is right, Gunther," came a cry from someone at the back of the room. "We've been hit and hit hard. Now what are we going to do about it?"

Murmurs of discontent filled the basement as many of the Rote-Abend terrorists expressed their anger and frustration. Heisler waited for them to vent their feelings, then raised his right hand for silence and continued.

"Do not think for a moment that the deaths of our friends will not be avenged. Of course those responsible will pay dearly. Unless we want Rote Abend to become the laughingstock of all Europe, we must strike back at the cowardly murderers who launched this unprovoked attack on us."

"But that's impossible," someone objected. "How can we retaliate without knowing where to point our guns?"

Heisler smiled. "That has never stopped us before, has it? Nor shall it now. We will simply choose any suitable target and then hit that target. Later we will issue a statement informing the media why the hit was made. That way we don't have to know the identity of our foes and they will still feel the sting of our blows."

"What about what Rupp said?" a man named Schiller questioned. "I don't know about the rest of you, but it disturbs me to think that we lost all our people at the factory to a force only five or six men strong."

"It would worry me, too," Heisler quickly confessed, "if I failed to consider where this information came from. We have all seen Rupp and listened to his story. He's upstairs bleeding to death right now and delirious with pain. By his own admission he couldn't see a damn thing when the bullets started flying, only vague shadows. And it was even darker inside the factory. He could not possibly know the number of attackers. If he had been close enough to keep count, he would not have lived long enough to escape the scene."

"I guess that's right," Schiller said. "I know I wouldn't stop to count heads if someone were shooting at me."

"Exactly," Heisler said. "And you can bet Rupp didn't stop, either."

"Does Gregor Churatov know about our loss of life and property?" Hans Driemann asked.

Heisler had anticipated the question. "Our brother from Moscow has not yet been informed of the trouble at the factory," Heisler reported. "I do not intend that he should know about it until we have retaliated."

"A wise decision." Ilse Stern backed Heisler up. "We must always remember that we need Churatov's financial support to make ends meet, and the last thing we want is for him, or his superiors, to consider payments to Rote Abend as money poorly spent."

"Ilse's point cannot be overemphasized," Heisler said. "For some time now, we have reaped the rewards of Churatov's sponsorship. Never mind that Churatov is a Communist. I would not care if he were the devil himself. Rote Abend's continued existence depends on keeping Churatov happy. Many of our competitors would jump at the chance to have the financing we have, and as long as Churatov is passing out the money, then let us make sure Rote Abend is first in line to receive it."

"Which takes us back to the matter of a retaliatory strike," Schiller said. "We all know that the strike has to be made. The only question is of when and where."

"No problem," Heisler responded. "If we put our heads together on this, I'm certain we'll come up with something appropriate."

"So am I, Gunther," Ilse Stern said.

9

Saturday morning found Phoenix Force and Dieter Beck gathered around a table at Beck's favorite café, eating a hearty breakfast of scrambled eggs, bacon, and rolls with butter while they discussed their progress in finding Karl Hahn.

Blue-black clouds hung over the city like great puffy bruises. There was more than a promise of rain in the air, and heavy thunderstorms before noon had been forecast.

"Lovely weather," David McCarter observed, munching on a piece of bacon as he looked out the window. "Tell me, Dieter, when does your summer officially arrive?"

"In July," Beck answered. "Second Tuesday of the month."

"And how long does the warm weather last?" quizzed the cockney.

"Until midnight that day."

"As long as that?" McCarter raised an eyebrow. "Sounds like summer in England."

Following their encounter with the Rote-Abend terrorists at the Stern Gerätfabrik, Dieter Beck had located a telephone and Gary Manning had called in an anonymous tip to the BKA. The Canadian stayed on the line only long enough to inform Beck's associates that several Rote Abend had been killed in the factory.

Then, from a hillside overlooking the factory, Phoenix Force and Beck had watched as six police cars entered the gates of the closed-down manufacturing plant and BKA officers swarmed into the factory building. Satisfied that Manning's call had been taken seriously, the Stony-Man five and their West-German host had devoted the rest of the night to trying to uncover a second Rote-Abend nest. Despite their best efforts, however, they had been unsuccessful. Shortly after dawn everyone had agreed they should have breakfast.

"I'm glad to see that last night's adventure has not made the headlines of this morning's paper," Yakov Katzenelenbogen observed as they ate. "And we heard nothing about it on the car radio, either."

"There won't be any undesirable publicity," Beck assured him, setting down his coffee cup. "It is no accident that we are considered among the most efficient police organizations in the world. It's standard BKA policy to reveal nothing about an ongoing or even a past investigation unless we are forced to do so.

Even then the information we supply would scarcely cover one corner of a postage stamp.

"We of the BKA are a tight-lipped lot. We refuse official interviews and routinely deny anything the media believe they have learned. When it comes to the serious business of crime solving, publicity can often get in the way of justice."

"No kidding," James said. "For a while there back home it almost seemed as if some criminals were selling the movie rights to their life stories before they committed their crimes. Weird. These animals would go out and murder someone, and then turn around and be paid by some publisher or film company for supplying all the grisly details. Fortunately the laws have been changed since, so that it's illegal now for criminals to profit from their crimes."

"But as you say," Encizo added, "it all comes back to publicity. Criminals have to be treated as criminals, instead of celebrities and media darlings if law enforcement personnel are going to be able to do a good job."

"Speaking of which," Gary Manning said, "what's our next move? We set Rote Abend back on their heels at the factory, which is all very well, but it doesn't bring us one step closer to learning where Hahn's being held prisoner.

"We're already into Saturday, and Monday will be here before we know it, and the zero hour for Hahn's execution. If the countdown is nail-biting time for us, you can imagine what it's like from Hahn's corner, especially if he knows that the man he's supposed to be exchanged for is dead. Damn!''

"One thing for sure," Katz said, "the more I learn about Rote Abend, the less I like."

"Do you mean the cylinder of isopropanol we discovered?" Beck asked, figuring Katz was concerned about the same thing he was.

"Yes," Katz admitted. "Instability among terrorist factions is well documented. Anything can set the bastards off. Knowing, as we do, what kind of horror Red Evening is capable of cooking up, well, it scares the hell out of me."

"Especially," James added, "when you stop and think that the storehouse of weapons we found was probably only one of many such caches. If they've spread their guns and ammunition around town, then it figures that there are more cylinders of isopropanol out there."

"Precisely," Katz said. "And why would they have isopropanol unless they intend, at some point, to manufacture GB?"

The GB the Israeli colonel referred to was a non-persistent G-series nerve agent, also known as Sarin, that was first produced in Germany in 1937. Sarin kills its victims by preventing the body's nerve synapses from firing properly, which leads to paralysis of the respiratory system and death by asphyxiation. Colorless, odorless and tasteless, sarin is disseminated as a vapor or liquid. Absorbed through the skin, it can kill within a half hour; direct inhalation of the gaseous form of the deadly nerve agent causes death in ten minutes or less.

"Maybe we should count our blessings and be grateful that Rote Abend went the binary route, instead of taking the unitary road to production," Manning offered. "Otherwise they might have been tempted to use the stuff before now."

"You could be right," Katz said. "On the other hand, once they decide it's time to act, it's not going to take them a year and a day to put the binary program to work. All they have to do is combine the isopropanol with the required second chemical component, and they're in business—instant GB, and potentially instant pain, suffering and the deaths of thousands, perhaps even millions of innocent people, depending upon how much of the nerve agent they plan to release. If Rote Abend is insane enough to fool around with producing GB, then they are capable of anything."

The binary concept of manufacturing chemical munitions had been gaining favor for some time because of its greater safety up to the point of use against an enemy. Binary munitions did not become lethal until two industrial grade chemicals combined inflight, after firing.

"Rote Abend is dangerous, there's no doubt about it," Beck said, as he drained his coffee cup. "Discovering that Gunther Heisler and his band of lunatics may be planning to unleash this GB nerve agent certainly adds a new dimension to our task. Unfortunately it moves the rescue of Karl Hahn to a lower rung on the ladder of priorities.''

"Whose priorities?" snapped McCarter. "Yours or ours?"

"Do not misunderstand," Beck said sincerely. "I want to save Hahn's life as much as you do. Even so, common sense dictates that the life of one man is less important than the lives of many. I don't know each of you as well as I do Manning here, but I am confident each of you would gladly sacrifice your own life if doing so would mean sparing the lives of countless innocents.'' The BKA agent looked McCarter straight in the eye. "Am I wrong, Herr Black?"

"No," the Briton answered without hesitation. "And Karl would say the same thing, I know. But if we can crack this Rote-Abend outfit wide open, then perhaps we can do both—save Hahn *and* stop Heisler and his men from using the GB."

"No argument there, my friend," Beck said, pushing away from the table. "Gentlemen?"

A minute later, as the six men stood beside Beck's Saab 900 discussing where to go next, the two-way radio inside the Saab came to life. Catching a phrase in the transmission, Beck unlocked the door quickly, but the desperate message being broadcast had already reached its conclusion and died.

The horror in the voice at the other end of the radio, however, had told Beck and Phoenix Force all they needed to know. That and the three words Beck had heard: *Innenstadt* and *Rote Abend*.

10

Bonn's Innenstadt, or city center, like those of most large metropolitan areas, is a hive of activity all day long, swarming with motor traffic and pedestrians. Four busy avenues radiate from the triangular hub and on all sides of the Innenstadt rise buildings four and five stories high, whose ground floors house a variety of stores and services. Bakeries, restaurants, butcher shops, department stores and an open-air market attract crowds to this busy urban location.

Rote Abend had not come to the city center to shop, a fact that was brutally evident as Phoenix Force and Dieter Beck raced onto the scene in their Saab and Volkswagen Quantum. Even before they reached the Innenstadt, they could easily see something was wrong.

Crowds of people, most of them on foot, charged up the street that Phoenix Force and Beck were trying to drive down. Locked in the steely grip of panic, their anxious faces painted with fear, the pedestrians were fleeing for their lives.

Beck was forced to cut the wheels of the Saab hard to the right to avoid a man who, clutching a bleeding shoulder wound, darted unexpectedly from the sidewalk into the path of the car. The Saab missed the injured man by inches and so did the Phoenix crew's rented Quantum sedan, driven by McCarter. By then they could hear the unmistakable cracking of autofire coming from the direction they were heading in.

Despite the crowds, the Saab 900 and the Volkswagen roared into the intersection of the Innenstadt like a couple of race cars speeding toward the finish line. Both vehicles turned left and sped along a road sandwiched between open-air market stalls on one side and a row of stores on the other.

Everywhere they looked the newcomers saw frightened shoppers and merchants huddling in doorways and even cowering in the open, trying to avoid being targets for the indiscriminate barrage of bullets that had transformed their Saturday morning into a nightmare. The bodies of an elderly man and woman were sprawled on the pavement next to a fresh vegetable stand. A couple of teenage boys also lay dead beside an overturned motorbike. One youth had been gunned down with a shot to the back, while most of the second victim's head seemed to be floating in a pool of blood.

"Scheiss!" Beck swore as more bodies could be seen on all sides. "Rote Abend's used these people for target practice."

"Just get us close enough," said Manning, his voice full of anger. "Then it's our turn."

Since they had heard the first announcement on Beck's radio after breakfast in the café, the emergency call had not been repeated. As the Saab and Quantum flew past the row of market stalls and entered the heart of the Innenstadt, the reason for the disturbing radio silence was obvious.

Two West-German police cars were parked nose to nose in the middle of the Innenstadt, their doors thrown open. The bodies of three *Schutzpolizei* sprawled on the pavement, moss-green tunics and beige trousers splattered in red. A fourth murdered policeman hung half in and half out of one vehicle, the coiled wire of a two-way radio microphone wrapped around his bloodied wrist.

In front of the police cars and next to a blue Mercedes van stood about a dozen Rote-Abend terrorists, armed to the teeth and drunk on the thrill of gunning down helpless citizens for kicks.

"Hang tight!" Beck warned Manning, and then the BKA agent brought the Saab 900 to a rubber-burning stop less than thirty yards from where the terrorists were gathered.

Faster than Beck had ever seen him move, Gary Manning was out of the Saab and settling some overdue debts with his Desert Eagle .357 Magnum.

First to feel the Eagle's sting was the man responsible for the deaths of the policemen. The trigger-happy goon was just about to use the bodies for target practice, when a double dose of Magnum-sized hell ripped into his chest and knocked him off his feet in a blistering fit of pain. Shrieking as he fell to the ground, the dying terrorist rid his pistol of its last bullet, firing the handgun with unerring accuracy into the stomach of the Rote-Abend killer to his right. The gut-shot thug swiftly followed his unintentional executioner to hell.

By then Dieter Beck was out of the Saab, too, and, standing to Manning's left, he began firing at the terrorists with his H&K MP-5 machine pistol. The remaining gun-toting terrorists, eight men and two women, quickly became aware that some extremely unwelcome visitors had arrived to spoil their party.

Unaccustomed to being on the receiving end of speeding bullets, the ten terrorists broke rank and ran. Some leaped into their parked Merc van to try to escape, while a half dozen or so Rote-Abend killers scattered toward the open-air marketplace nearby, where any shots fired at them as they fled would risk hitting the farmers and shoppers hiding among the stalls.

"Roundabout time," McCarter warned his mates in the Quantum. Then he slammed on the brakes, at the same time powerfully spinning the steering wheel to the right.

The VW sedan slid forward in response to McCarter's expert skills as a driver and rolled into the turn. The white-knuckled passengers shifted first to the right and then to the left as McCarter brought the car out of the about-face maneuver. Aimed now where he wanted to go, the former pride of the SAS sent the Quantum rocketing toward the marketplace stalls directly ahead.

Before the VW had traveled fifty feet, one of the Rote-Abend terrorists racing for the stalls turned and opened fire with his Socimi Type 821 submachine gun. There were two loud explosions as the Quantum's front tires were hit, and suddenly McCarter was driving on rims.

"End of the ride," the Londoner announced, as he successfully braked and steered the sedan to a rocky stop. "Let's show them what we're made of!"

The Volkswagen's doors opened at once and the four Phoenix soldiers emerged to confront their Rote-Abend foes. As a wave of lead from Encizo's MP-5 blistered the gunman who had shot the tires, the guy seemed stunned that his Italian subgun had failed to save his life. The terrorist's face was erased in a flash of blinding light.

Any ideas the dead man's friends might have entertained about launching an assault against the four armed strangers from the Quantum evaporated in a puff of despair when they saw one of their own cut down before their eyes.

Ilse Stern was stunned. Like many of her fellow terrorists, she had begun to think she and her associates were invincible. But now Rote Abend's day of reckoning seemed to be at hand. The first order of business was to stay alive, and while those armed interlopers were on the loose, she for one was going to hide in the marketplace stalls.

"Come!" the woman who was Gunther Heisler's lover called to her associates. "Standing here in the open is inviting disaster."

Without waiting to see if they were following her, Ilse Stern turned and ran for her life.

Not all the Rote-Abend terrorists scattered and ran. While several killers raced for the market stalls, and three fled to the Mercedes van, one of the gunmen making for the Merc suddenly stopped dead in his tracks and turned. He aimed his Star Z-70 submachine gun at Gary Manning.

Though armed with his .357 Eagle, the Canadian recognized a lopsided contest when he saw one. As the Rote-Abend assassin prepared to fire his Spanish subgun, Manning spun swiftly and dived over the hood of the Saab, clearing the left front fender and hitting the ground just as the Star Z-70's 9 mm song began to play.

With lead hammering a metallic rhythm on the Saab's frame, Manning worried that the hoodlum, deprived of one target, would turn the Star SMG on Dieter Beck. A heartbeat later the Z-70's music abruptly stopped, and to Manning's relief Beck shouted to him that it was safe to surface. The BKA officer had wielded his H&K MP-5 against the Z-70 gunman, who lay on his back, dead, his vacant eyes staring at the sky, his body riddled with holes.

Manning and Beck then wasted no time stopping two more German terrorists.

The front doors of the Mercedes van were open, with the Rote-Abend duo about to jump inside, when Manning called to them in German to stop and lay down their guns.

"Halt!" he shouted. *"Legen die Waffen nieder!"*

Since he and Beck had their weapons trained on the Red-Evening foes at a distance of less than fifteen yards, Manning hoped they would see the futility of resisting and surrender. Phoenix Force needed information if they were to locate and save Hahn, as well as discover what Rote Abend intended to do with the GB nerve agent known as sarin. To get that information, it was crucial that a prisoner be taken.

Neither of the Rote-Abend killers, however, obeyed Manning's order. Her face masked with anger, the raven-haired woman climbing behind the wheel of the van tried to aim her automatic rifle. The cramped quarters slowed her down. She was still fumbling with her gun when Manning's .357 beat her to the punch, obliterating her face. Rocked off her feet by the force of the blast, the dead terrorist's rifle went flying, and so did she.

The killer on the other side of the van yelled out about freedom and his willingness to die for a noble cause, then with his MAS 5.56 held out before him, he broke away from the Merc and charged straight for Manning and Beck. But the rifleman was only a few steps into his attack when Beck's MP-5 erupted with a three-round burst.

One of the BKA operative's shots tore a harmless path through the terrorist's coat sleeve, but the final two slugs from the Heckler and Koch struck the charging madman in the upper left side of his chest crashing through his rib cage to shred his heart and lungs. The terrorist stumbled and, dead in seconds, nose-dived to the pavement.

Scarcely had the dead man's body hit the dirt when a new wave of gunfire sounded from the direction of the Innenstadt market stalls. Wordlessly Manning and Beck reloaded their weapons, then ran to join the fight.

11

For most of the year in the Federal Republic of Germany westerly winds and a temperate climate prevail. Continental conditions, or those where greater extremes in temperatures exist between day and night and between summer and winter, are experienced increasingly inland and to the south. Precipitation usually ranges between twenty-four and thirty inches a year.

For this reason the stalls of the open-air market in Bonn's Innenstadt were covered by oversize umbrellas and broad canopies of terra-cotta-colored canvas, to protect shoppers and merchants from the often chilling rain. Yakov Katzenelenbogen and his three Stony-Man sidekicks, however, wasted no time wondering if the canvas roof over their heads would leak in a rainstorm. They had seen six Rote-Abend terrorists flee into the tarp-covered area of the Innenstadt, and were bent on tracking down the killers.

The Rote-Abend six had been less than thirty seconds ahead of Phoenix Force, but had put the scant lead to good use. Because of the heavy clouds, it was dim and gloomy beneath the canvas enclosure. Nowhere within the outdoor shopping facility could a terrorist be seen. The market seemed to have swallowed them whole.

The fifty stalls were arranged in five rows, each ten stalls deep. Aisles, some as wide as ten feet, crisscrossed between the stalls. Katz motioned for his men to take one aisle each and sweep from one end to the other. In addition to the 9 mm Uzi submachine gun carried by the one-armed Israeli commando, Encizo carried an MP-5, McCarter an Ingram MAC-10 and Calvin an S&W M-76 subgun.

Wary that the six Rote-Abend adversaries might attack all at once, and with the sound of the gunfight involving Manning and Beck in the distance, each of the four Phoenix-Force mates jogged to the end of the rows they were to search and launched their sweep up the aisles.

ILSE STERN RAN a third of the way up the market aisle before she ducked into a deserted booth specializing in shoes for the family and dropped to her hands and knees. Then she began to crawl in the same direction she had been running.

The female terrorist swallowed the lump in her throat and wondered anxiously if the rapid beat of her heat was as loud as she imagined. Could anyone else hear it? Of course not, she convinced herself, but the lingering doubt remained. Fear was a new experience for Ilse, and she did not like it.

As she carried her Beretta M-12 submachine gun in her hand and awkwardly crawled from the stall she was in to the next one in line, she knew she had every reason to be afraid. How many Rote Abend had lost their lives in the past few minutes? she wondered. With the muffled shots continuing to come from where the terrorists had parked their van, she was sure the death toll would be even higher.

Ilse's intuition told her that the men pursuing her now were the same ones who had attacked William Rupp and the others at the factory the night before. Who else could they be? But if they were the same men, who were they working for? If not the BND, the BfV or the BKA, then who?

Not knowing the identity of the adversaries heightened Ilse's dread. She knew that the individual rights of all citizens in the Federal Republic of Germany were guaranteed and protected by the constitution. This Basic Law, or *Grundgesetz*, meant that suspects could not be forced to talk to the police. Also, subjecting suspects to physical abuse, torture, deceit, drugs, or hypnosis was illegal. Arrests could be made using only the minimum force necessary. But if the men chasing Ilse Stern and her friends now were not with the regular police, they were not bound to obey the *Grundgesetz*, she reasoned. Even if she was not killed but taken prisoner, she knew that she, and all the Rote-Abend members, would still be in grave danger.

Something tapped the calf of Ilse's right leg and she gasped, stifling a scream. She turned, brought her M-12 around, ready to fire, but held off when she recognized Martin Lessing, also on his hands and knees, with a finger to his lips. She nodded, then motioned him nearer so she could whisper in his ear.

"Where are the others?" she asked.

"Arendt and Grebing are hiding in a stall across the aisle from us," came the barely audible answer.

"What about Bleek and Nolte?"

Lessing shrugged and shook his head.

"We must escape," the woman said, pointing in the direction she had been going. "It is our only hope, Martin. Our enemies will kill us if they find us, and I am not ready to die. Come."

Without another word Ilse Stern began to crawl from stall to stall again, but this time not alone.

12

Manfred Bleek did not believe in omens. Only fools were superstitious, he often stated. Even so, the terrorist had to acknowledge to himself, someone with considerable pull where it counted must be looking out for his best interests in this tight situation he was in, and Bleek couldn't have been happier about it.

Walking toward Bleek now was an easy mark, a pushover to delight any bloodthirsty terrorist. The target was an overweight one-armed gunman who, in the dimness of the canopied aisle, seemed only to lack a walking cane to complete the picture of an old man past his prime. Killing him would be a cinch.

Bleek would have loved nothing more than to pump the old boy full of holes, but the uproar would alert the old man's friends, and Bleek had no desire to take on all of them at once. Better to kill him in silence and be done with it.

The market stall Bleek was hiding in was a bargain hunter's delight. Something for Everyone, a Banner stretched over the front of the booth announced, and the wares on display came close to living up to the advertised claim.

The stall was living proof that one man's trash was another man's treasure. Its merchandise included drinking straws that were red plastic spirals, candle holders standing on top of miniature No Smoking signs, copper teakettles, brush-and-comb sets, raincoats and seasonal sporting goods. Most interesting to Bleek was a rack of aluminum ski poles.

Taking one of the poles in his hand and deciding it would make a good weapon, Bleek hid in back of a row of raincoats and waited for his victim to come within range. If he handled the hit correctly, he could play pincushion with the one-armed man without making a sound, and then be off before anyone else was aware the old man was dead.

Honor, by Bleek's definition, was what fools ate for lunch; when it came time to attack, Bleek would not think twice about stabbing his foe in the back, sinking the point of the pole into flesh clear up to its snow ring. What the hell was the old goat going to do? File a complaint? Nobody ever said life was fair, so as soon as the old man walked past the stall, Bleek would strike.

Katz sensed the attack coming at him from behind an instant before he whirled and actually saw the pointed end of the ski pole driving directly toward his heart. Instinctively the Israeli raised his left hand, which held the Uzi. As the point stabbed at him, Katz slid the Uzi beneath the aluminum shaft, pushing out and up. Then suddenly the Red-Evening terrorist let go of the pole.

With the resistance of the ski pole gone, Katz was thrown off balance and leaned backward to take most of his weight on his right leg. Before Katz could fully recover the killer struck again, using another ski pole he had pulled from his arsenal inside the stall where he had been hiding.

This time the killer tried to slash the deadly pole down on Katzenelenbogen's head. Katz's left hand, holding the Uzi, shot up, and the pole bent as it connected with the Israeli's gun. The killer yelped painfully and the pole was torn from his grasp. The fight wasn't over, though, because Katz, too, lost his grip on the Uzi.

When he saw his victim's submachine gun fall to the ground, the killer quickly drew a wicked-looking knife from a sheath he wore on his belt. He lunged at Katz and the Israeli felt the keen edge of the blade slice harmlessly through the fabric of his coat as he jumped back.

Katz twisted and smashed down his hooked prosthesis on top of the killer's forearm. The Rote-Abend hood grunted and his fingers opened, dropping his knife. Before he could grab it again Katz's left fist stunned the would-be assassin with a rock-solid punch to the side of the face.

The terrorist swore and shook his head in fury, then shoved the prosthesis aside and leaped straight at Katz, locking his hands around the Israeli's throat. Katz's eyes bulged as the terrorist applied enough pressure to squeeze teardrops from stone, grinning from ear to ear.

"Say your prayers, old man," the killer advised with a sneer. "It is time for you to die."

But Katz thought otherwise. He swung his prosthesis and deftly inserted one of its three hooks into the killer's smiling mouth. Katz shoved in the hook as far as he could, then flexed the stump of his right arm to bring the three prongs together.

An unholy scream of agony bubbled from the killer as his smile was rinsed with blood and the left side of his face was torn away. The fingers clamped on Katz's throat relaxed, releasing their tenacious grip. The Phoenix team's unit commander manipulated his prosthesis, and a chunk of red flesh fell from the bloodied hooks.

Mad with pain, and beyond caring who heard him fire his submachine gun, the killer reached for and found his weapon, swinging it into play just as Katz swept his Uzi off the pavement and put the Rote-Abend fanatic out of his misery forever. Four 9 mm parabellum bullets slammed one after another into the killer's torso, knocking him off his feet and sending him backpedaling into a carefully arrange display of candle holders. The killer's body twitched a little after he fell, then was still.

Shots rang out from what Katz recognized as Encizo's MP-5 a second before the dead body of another Rote-Abend bad guy tumbled into the aisle a few feet away from Katz.

"Thanks," Katz said, as Encizo stepped into the open from behind the canvas partition separating two booths. Then both men turned to the sound of Manning and Dieter Beck rushing up the aisle.

"What's the good word?" Manning asked.

"We're still in one piece," Encizo told him.

"And the rest of your team?" Beck inquired.

The abrupt chatter of James's M-76 SMG answered Beck's question.

IF ILSE STERN AND HER FRIENDS had any illusions about crawling to safety on their hands and knees, they quickly vanished as Manfred Bleek's nerve-chilling screams reached their ears.

"God!" Lessing exclaimed. "They've got Bleek!"

"And they're not getting us!" vowed the female terrorist. "Follow me."

Without waiting for Lessing, Stern leaped to her feet and darted from the stall she was in to the aisle nearby. There Lessing joined her, and finally Grebing and Arendt. The woman shuddered. Only four left from their original twelve. What a miserable performance on their part! Gunther would be furious.

"What is that?" Grebing shouted, raising his assault rifle to investigate.

Then a submachine gun began firing. In the blink of an eye Ernst Grebing ceased to exist, peppered by a string of bullets that brought him to his knees, then knocked him forward flat on his face.

Leaving their dead comrade behind, the three remaining Red-Evening killers charged to the end of the aisle, breaking into the open from the canvas-covered area, desperately scanning from left to right to find any way to escape. Ilse Stern found what she was searching for.

A gray-haired man in his fifties was cowering behind the wheel of his Mitsubishi sedan, parked on the edge of the Innenstadt. As the terrorist trio advanced on him at gunpoint he was too afraid to move or drive away.

"Out!" Stern waved her Beretta M-12 SMG in the sedan owner's face. "Leave the keys in the ignition. Hurry, or I'll shoot."

Tears rolled down the frightened man's cheeks as he opened his car door and did as he was told. "Please," he begged through trembling lips. "My invalid wife needs me. Please don't hurt me."

Ilse Stern nodded to Lessing. "You drive," she said. Then she pointed her Beretta at the old man's head and blew away the top of his skull. She climbed in next to Lessing, while Georg Arendt jumped into the back of the car. "If he was all his wife had going for her, she's better off without him. Get us the hell out of here!''

Lessing started the engine and shifted into gear, flooring the accelerator while releasing the clutch. The Mitsubishi four-door seemed to leap off the street as its wheels gained traction and sent the sedan speeding away from the city-center complex and the site of Rote Abend's ignoble defeat.

David McCarter emerged from the Innenstadt's canopied stalls just in time to see the Mitsubishi sedan carrying his escaping enemies whip around a corner and disappear up a street in the direction of the Rhine. The disgusted cockney considered his unfired Ingram for a moment, then noticed a woman's head peering cautiously over the steering wheel of a jet-black Maserati Biturbo that looked as if it had just been driven off the showroom floor.

McCarter's face brightened. He ran for the Maserati, apparently terrifying the woman at the wheel. She screamed, jumped out of the car and fled on foot, waving her hands wildly and shrieking as she ran.

McCarter quickly checked that the keys were in the ignition and shouted a sincere *"Danke!"* to the retreating owner of the Maserati, then lowered himself behind the wheel and started the engine.

As the British commando released the hand brake, Gary Manning ran out from another section of the tarp-covered stalls. McCarter burned rubber screeching across the pavement to Manning, where he stopped long enough to pop open the door on the passenger side.

"Where'd you get the wheels?" Manning asked.

"A nice German lady let me borrow it," McCarter replied, then added in a tone all too familiar to Manning, "Hop in, mate. We're going for a ride."

13

McCarter and Manning crossed the Rhine River on the Kennedy Bridge at what Manning thought must be close to the speed of sound.

"Imagine," McCarter commented, "the Rhine carries more traffic than any other waterway in the world."

"Thanks for telling me," Manning said dryly. "I want to savor this moment. I can tell my grandchildren that viewing the Rhine with you was the most frightening experience of my life."

"Rubbish!" McCarter said. "How can we catch up to the three Rote Abend who got away if we don't drive fast?"

"If this car had wings, we'd be in orbit by now." The Canadian tensed as McCarter accelerated to pass a slower-moving Porsche. "Besides, you're not even sure this is the way the terrorists went."

"Who says I'm not sure?"

"Okay, then where are they? Point them out."

"I will."

"When?"

"Soon."

"How soon?"

"Please," McCarter begged, "how can I concentrate on my driving if you keep asking all these questions?"

"How can I concentrate on my questions if you keep driving like this?"

"We'll ask Katz to explain it when we see him," the Londoner answered. "In the meantime, I think we'll head for the autobahn. It's the fastest way out of the city, which I'm betting will suit the Red-Evening killers we're chasing just fine. They're going to want to put as much distance between them and the city center as possible."

"That could be the ticket they'd shoot for," Manning agreed. "Especially since the autobahn has no set speed limits."

McCarter looked at Manning and smiled. "I know."

"Say they take the autobahn, then. Which direction do you think they'll go?"

"My guess says north toward the airport."

"And they're driving a Mitsubishi?"

"That's right. A sedan the color of chocolate. Any more questions?"

"Just one," Manning said, pointing. "Is that them?"

McCarter responded by feeding more fuel to the Maserati's engine.

"DAMN!" GEORG ARENDT SWORE. "Never in my life have I been so humiliated. Poor Grebing and I were made to crawl about on our hands and knees like dogs."

"So were we," Lessing said from behind the wheel of the Mitsubishi. "All we needed were bones in our mouths to make the image complete."

"Stop complaining, both of you," Ilse Stern said. "Be grateful we escaped with our lives. We left many of our good friends back at the city center. We are fortunate it wasn't all of us."

"First last night at the factory, and now this," Lessing said with a sigh. "Any more bad luck and our reputation will be completely destroyed."

"You're wrong, Lessing," Arendt said. "These past two days we've had enough shit dumped on us to keep a plumber busy for the rest of his life."

"I wouldn't let Gunther hear you say that," the woman advised. "You know how much he hates negativity."

"Don't let your relationship with Gunther blind you to the truth, Ilse," Arendt said. "Red Evening has never had its ass beaten so badly before and you know it. How many comrades have we lost since last night? More than twenty-five? That's not negativity, Ilse. It's facing reality."

"We're coming up to the A170," Lessing interrupted, referring to the autobahn. "Which way should we go?"

Arendt spoke first. "I say to the south."

"Ridiculous," Ilse Stern scoffed. "Drive to the south and they will capture us for sure."

"That's only if someone saw us steal this car," Arendt countered. "If they did not, then we are home free."

"A risk I'm not willing to take," Stern argued. "The repercussions of today's dismal adventure may be far-reaching. Perhaps no one did see us take this car; I don't know. But if there is even one witness to tell the police about it, then we are in trouble. They would be onto us before we could make it to Koblenz."

"So, it's the airport, is it?" Lessing inquired.

"Yes, to the airport," Lessing's female passenger repeated. "We will ditch the car there along with our guns, then each take a different flight out of the area. We will fly back only after we have telephoned Gunther and he has assured us that it is safe to return. It may seem overcautious, I know, but . . ."

"Better safe than sorry," Lessing said, slowing for the approach to the A170, then following a line of cars onto the autobahn. "It has been several weeks since I was in Paris. I think I will try to fly. . ." Lessing halted in midsentence as his eyes probed the reflection in the rearview mirror.

"What is it?" Ilse asked, immediately sensing something was wrong.

"It may be nothing," Lessing told her, "but there is a car behind us that I think I saw in the city center."

The other two terrorists turned in their seats for a look.

"Which one?" Arendt questioned.

"The Biturbo about six cars back," Lessing said.

"I see it," Arendt said. "The shiny black one?"

"That's it," Lessing answered. "I'm sure it's the same one."

Stern tightened the shoulder strap of her seat belt and stroked the Beretta M-12 submachine gun resting on her lap. "Well, there's one way to find out, now, isn't there?"

"THEY'VE SPOTTED US," McCarter said, watching the Mitsubishi suddenly veer to the left and race ahead of the row of cars entering the autobahn. The Briton hit the Maserati's turn indicator, pulling to the left, also, and gunning the engine. "What do you say we go catch them?"

Manning was skeptical. "Do I have a choice?"

"That's the spirit."

The Mitsubishi's response to McCarter's maneuver was instantaneous. The Japanese import carrying the trio of Rote-Abend terrorists leaped forward, cutting in front of a Peugeot station wagon. As soon as the stolen car cleared the Peugeot, it increased its speed and left the wagon behind.

"So that's the way they want to play the game," McCarter observed. Before Manning could protest, the former SAS commando had pulled alongside the Peugeot to try to follow in the Mitsubishi's wake.

But the driver of the station wagon refused to cooperate. He had already suffered the indignity of having one car cut in front of him; he wasn't about to let it happen again. As the Maserati next to him sped up, so did the Peugeot.

"He's not going to let us by," Manning said as he watched the Rote Abend's Mitsubishi disappear around a curve in the autobahn. "And there go the terrorists."

The front bumper of the Maserati was now nearly touching the rear bumper of a Mercedes-Benz 560-SEL sedan. To the right the Peugeot paced even.

"Not to worry," McCarter told Manning. "I'm sure the driver in the wagon will listen to reason. I'll just give him a few beeps on the hooter, while you wave him to slow down and get out of our way."

"As easy as that?" Manning said.

"Sure," McCarter replied enthusiastically. "European drivers are renowned for their courtesy on the highway."

But after McCarter hooted and Manning waved, the driver of the Peugeot still refused to budge.

"So much for the renowned courtesy of European drivers." Manning said. "What now?"

"Now," McCarter explained, "we try the direct approach."

The direct approach involved McCarter's easing the Maserati across its lane and into that of the Peugeot until the sides of the cars were practically touching. The driver of the Peugeot observed the Briton's action with indifference, his smug expression as he glanced at McCarter almost daring the cockney to come any closer.

"I guess it's time for an even more direct approach," McCarter decided.

The next thing Manning knew, McCarter bumped the right side of the Maserati against the left side of the Peugeot, not so hard as to run the French station wagon off the autobahn, but hard enough to show the other driver that McCarter was serious about the Peugeot slowing down and letting him pass. He slapped the Maserati against the Peugeot a second time, and finally the station wagon's driver got the message.

Before McCarter could repeat his experiment in nonverbal communication, the driver of the Peugeot shook his fist in anger, but reduced his speed sufficiently to permit the Maserati to cut in front of him and continue on its way.

McCarter expressed his gratitude by waving his hand out the window at the fuming driver. Then he asked Manning, "Where were we?"

"That's some roadside manner you've got there, Doctor," Manning said as McCarter weaved in and out of autobahn traffic like a flea through the fur of its favorite dog. "I hope the lady who loaned you this car back at the Innenstadt won't be too upset at what you've done to her paint job."

"Not a chance," McCarter assured the Canadian. "She's too much of a sweetheart to let a little body-work come between us."

They were five kilometers from Bonn Airport when McCarter and Manning finally caught up to their Rote-Abend adversaries. By then the rain that had been predicted had started to fall in a light drizzle, making the surface of the autobahn shiny and slick. Because he was determined not to lose the terrorists again, McCarter soon had the Maserati trailing directly behind the Japanese import they were chasing.

The Maserati's presence did not go unnoticed. The terrorists' first response was to try somehow to outrun the Italian pursuit car, a tactic that did not succeed.

McCarter whistled. "You know how fast we're going?"

"No, and don't tell me," Manning said.

"One hundred eighty kilometers," McCarter said anyway. "Just under one hundred and ten miles an hour."

The terrorist in the Mitsubishi's backseat rolled down his window and leaned out, a submachine gun in his hands.

"Oh, look," Manning said, lowering his own window. "Now *he's* trying the direct approach." Manning picked up McCarter's Ingram MAC-10, which was lying on the seat between them. "May I?"

Shifting his weight so he was hanging partway out the window of the Maserati, Manning was hit in the face with a spray of cold rain. He ignored the rain as he put the MAC-10 to work before the terrorist target let loose with his SMG.

At the distance separating the Canadian from the Rote-Abend gunman Manning could not miss, nor did he. Squeezing off a quarter of the Ingram's thirty-two-round magazine, the Phoenix-Force team's ace sniper made certain that all eight of the 9 mm parabellum rounds met their flesh-and-blood target.

The Red-Evening killer jerked and twitched each time he was hit, and his subgun fell to the roadway. He shuddered and slumped farther out the window, so that his fingers bounced along the autobahn like ten bony breadsticks. Then gravity prevailed and the terrorist's entire body spilled in a heap from the Mitsubishi window to the road.

McCarter expertly avoided the obstacle in his path, then said to Manning, "We can't afford to have them shooting at us on the autobahn. There's too much of a risk they'll miss us and kill somebody behind us."

"Yeah, you're right," Manning agreed. "And they wouldn't give a damn, either. Let's see how they manage with just three wheels."

Manning leaned out the Maserati's window again and aimed the durable Ingram just below the Mitsubishi's back bumper.

"Curve coming up to the left," McCarter advised.

Manning fired a triple burst of M-10 lead on a collision course with the Mitsubishi's right rear tire. The radial proved no match for the confrontation and exploded with a terrific boom, forcing the terrorists' vehicle to fishtail from side to side.

McCarter braked and slowed as the driver of the Mitsubishi failed to negotiate the autobahn's sweeping curve to the left and the car shot off the high-speed roadway at more than one hundred eighty kilometers an hour. A gentle incline rose just beyond the autobahn's shoulder and, upon hitting the low hill, the out-of-control Red-Evening car flipped over on its roof. It skidded upside down for a bumpy five seconds, then stopped.

McCarter pumped the brakes and brought the Maserati to rest on the shoulder of the autobahn, less than twenty meters from where the wreck of the Mitsubishi was already spewing a spiral of ominous black smoke. With his .357 Eagle locked in his fist, Manning sprang from the car, sprinting through the rain and mud to search for Rote-Abend survivors. By the time he reached the Mitsubishi, the single plume of black smoke had become three.

Manning ran to the driver's side of the import and bent down for a look in just as McCarter joined him. Inside the car the terrorist who had been driving was dangling like a rag doll from his still-fastened seat belt. The grotesque angle at which the man's head touched the steering wheel left no doubt that he had died from a broken neck.

"The other one's alive," McCarter shouted from the opposite side of the automobile, his MAC-10 submachine gun clutched in his right hand. "Just barely, but alive."

Then he reached into the vehicle and pulled the unconscious female terrorist free from the wreckage as carefully as he could. Manning helped him hurry things up after a whumping sound came from the trunk of the car, and the Mitsubishi started to burn.

"Run," McCarter yelled, as he and Manning, carrying their injured prisoner, raced to escape the impending explosion.

When the Mitsubishi's fuel tank erupted seconds later, the shock wave of the blast slammed into the retreating Phoenix pros from behind and knocked them off their feet. As they fell they instinctively extended their arms to prevent the Rote-Abend terrorist from being injured any more than she already was. A secondary explosion quickly followed the first. As McCarter and Manning shielded the terrorist's body with their own, a shower of shredded metal and plastic fell from the sky along with the rain.

When it was safe to do so, Manning and McCarter lifted their heads and looked back to survey the damage done to the Rote-Abend car. Destruction of the Mitsubishi sedan was total. While flames licked at the import's frame, McCarter smiled and nudged Manning in the ribs.

"Dandy," McCarter said. "We may be muddy and soaked to the skin, and we'll probably both come down with double pneumonia, but we're alive."

"Gee, one out of four's not bad when you look at it like that," Manning concurred. "Especially since we're not walking away from this empty-handed."

"Right. Well, let's get her to a hospital, then," said McCarter. "Now that we have her we don't want to lose her."

At that moment a half-dozen Mercedes-Benz West-German police cars, with blue emergency lights flashing and sirens screaming in unison, converged on the scene.

"Then again," Manning amended, letting his .357 drop to the ground, "maybe we already have."

14

Preliminary information on Rote Abend's disastrous strike at Bonn's city center was not difficult for Gunther Heisler to come by. Indeed, it was as easy as turning on the radio. Most of the stations were broadcasting accounts of the terrorist group's humiliating defeat, with on-the-spot teams of reporters interviewing police and survivors.

Heisler's mood darkened more with each new disclosure. By noon he was thoroughly sick to his stomach. The strike in retaliation for the attack at the factory the night before had backfired in their faces. Never, in Heisler's memory, had an operation gone so sour so fast.

How they could keep their Soviet benefactor, Gregor Churatov, from learning of the Innenstadt fiasco, Heisler had no idea. At least five of those slain at the city center had been tentatively identified by the police as Rote-Abend members in good standing. So far, Ilse had not been announced dead, but Heisler believed he would eventually hear her name among the list of victims.

The death toll of innocent bystanders was high, and some of the gravely wounded were expected to increase the final number. Already the cry for Rote-Abend blood rang loud and clear through the streets of Bonn.

Comrade Churatov would have to be vacationing on Mars to miss the excitement. Who could predict what the Communist's reaction might be? Perhaps he would go so far as to withdraw the financial support Rote Abend had enjoyed for so long. The idea of having to scrounge and beg again, as they had before Churatov made his bankroll available, was totally repugnant to Heisler.

Even more worrisome to the terrorist leader, as he paced back and forth in the meeting room in his home's converted basement, was that they still had not unmasked their mysterious opponents. As far as Heisler had been able to determine, the men responsible for killing his people were not associated with any of the Federal Republic of Germany's security forces. So who were they? How in the hell had so few of them been able to defeat so many Rote Abend? And without so much as a single reported casualty? To Heisler's way of thinking, the luck required for such an achievement defied calculation.

Not all of Heisler's knowledge of the latest setback was provided by radio news reports. An acquaintance of his, a man named Brunner, who was unaware of Heisler's Rote-Abend connection, owned a drugstore whose main entrance opened onto the Innenstadt. On the pretense of telephoning to see if Brunner had survived the widely publicized terrorist attack unharmed, Heisler had pumped the talkative druggist for whatever additional information the man could supply.

Brunner told Heisler he and his wife spent the period of the gun battle huddled with their customers on the floor of their shop, quivering with fear and praying for their lives. As soon as the shooting stopped and he determined it was safe, Brunner had peeked out his mercifully undamaged front window to observe the aftermath of the fight. Sprawled on the pavement nearby were the bodies of four murdered policemen, as well as five "Rote-Abend pigs." One dead terrorist, the druggist noted, was female; from the description Brunner supplied, Heisler knew, with relief, the body was not Ilse's.

Then Brunner's attention had been diverted from the bodies near his shop to four armed men, none of them wearing uniforms, who hurried from beneath the canopied merchant stalls toward a parked car. They had climbed inside, then driven away.

Brunner had noted nothing extraordinary about the armed strangers, except that the eldest had an artificial arm, and another was black. The vehicle had disappeared, and moments later the police had arrived.

Brunner had also explained to Heisler that his wife was making her statement to the police even as they spoke. He had ended their talk by thanking Heisler for thinking of him, then had said goodbye.

Heisler recalled his conversation with Brunner while staring forlornly at the empty seats of the meeting room. More than two dozen Rote-Abend revolution-aries had occupied those seats last night, yet in an hour, when their emergency meeting convened, only slightly more than half that number would attend.

At the rate Heisler's followers were dying off, Rote Abend would soon boast a membership of one, he was thinking grimly when the phone in the basement rang. Reluctantly Heisler lifted the receiver to his ear.

"Yes?"

"I believe we should talk."

Heisler's toes curled inside his shoes. It was Chur-atov. "You've heard the news, I suppose?" Dead silence greeted the question. "Of course, you have. Why else would you be calling?"

"Do you intend telling me what happened, or do I have to wait and read all about it in the newspaper?"

"We've never kept anything from you."

"Granted. And I don't expect you to start now. Go on. I'm listening."

"We had some trouble last night out at the factory. You know the one I mean."

"What kind of trouble?"

"We were hit by an unknown force, anywhere from four to six men. Only one of my people survived the confrontation, but we lost him in the middle of the night."

"And the merchandise from the factory? Did you lose that, too?"

"All of it."

"That could create a problem," Churatov said. "But go on. What about today?"

"It was a strike against the citizens of Bonn in retaliation for what happened at the factory. Since we didn't know who to blame for the attack, we decided to make everyone pay."

"Commendable, but aren't you jumping ahead of our timetable? Why wasn't I consulted before this retaliatory strike of yours took place?"

Heisler was almost too embarrassed to answer. "Because we didn't want to interrupt you while you were involved with your current project."

"Again commendable, but that's hardly the way things have turned out."

"I know," Heisler said.

"How many casualties are we talking about altogether?"

"Sixteen last night. Today I sent twelve. Since none have returned to home base I have to assume they are all dead."

"Not necessarily," Churatov said without explanation. "But what about those responsible for today's loss?"

"The evidence indicates that they are the same group we encountered at the factory."

"What evidence?"

Heisler informed Churatov of all he had learned from his talk with Brunner, up to and including the part about the enemy gunman with an artificial arm.

"Hmm." Churatov digested this last piece of news with mild surprise. "A one-armed man, you say?"

"Him and three others. Why? Don't tell me you know who he is?"

"Not exactly. But if he belongs to a certain fighting unit I know of, then it would explain much, especially how so few of them were able to eliminate so many of your colleagues. If this man is who I think he is, then the odds against him and his friends could have been many times higher, and they still would have come out on top."

"That's not very reassuring."

"Nor is it meant to be. You must be hurting for warm bodies right about now."

Heisler glanced to the roomful of empty chairs before him. "In the past two days we have lost two-thirds of our active members."

"But you have access to reserve forces in other cities throughout the country?"

"A dozen or so people I can count on, yes."

"Then it's time to call them in. Now. If you have not already realized it, this is a state of emergency. The one-armed man and his friends have declared war on you and your associates, and unless you are prepared to hit them with everything and everyone at your disposal, then I am afraid there will be no one left for me to deal with when payday rolls around next month."

"I thought as much," Heisler admitted honestly. "There is no point funding an organization that cannot protect itself."

"More important, my friend," Churatov replied coldly, "there is no way to take a dead man to dinner."

"Your advice is not wasted. I will call in my reserves as soon as we hang up."

"Splendid," Churatov said, then seemed to hesitate.

"There is more?" Heisler asked.

"Yes. You remember I said it is not definite that all of your people perished at the Innenstadt this morning?"

"Someone survived? Who?"

Churatov dropped the bombshell. "Ilse Stern."

"Ilse?" Heisler stammered his lover's name. "She's alive?"

"I believe so. She was injured in an automobile crash on the A170."

"This is incredible," Heisler said. "How did you learn of this?"

"How I learned it is unimportant. What does matter is that her capture represents a breach of security that we can ill afford at this time. I am aware that you and Fräulein Stern enjoyed a relationship, but we have a serious problem on our hands that cannot be ignored.

"I have no knowledge of the extent of her injuries, but if your Ilse recovers sufficiently, then she will be questioned. If questioned, she will talk. Such an interrogation must not take place. I cannot tolerate any interference with my plans for this weekend. Do I make myself clear?"

"As clear as crystal," Heisler said. "Where is Ilse now?"

Churatov gave the name of a local hospital. "She is in a private room under the protection of at least three armed guards."

"No matter. We shall orchestrate a rescue operation at once."

"Rescue? At what cost? Your ranks are already severely depleted. Even with the reserves you intend calling in, I don't see that you have enough people to spare to mount a successful rescue. Too much could go wrong. Forgive my frankness, but it makes no sense to risk the last of your resources to save a woman who is near death anyway."

"What do you suggest, then?" Heisler whispered.

"Send in one man. Your best. Send him to the hospital where Ilse Stern is being treated and . . ."

"And?"

"Terminate her. I am sorry, but it's the only way I see out of this dilemma. You do agree, of course?"

"And if I don't?"

"If you refuse to send in one of your people to do the job, then I will send in one of mine. The result will be the same in any event. Naturally, if I have to arrange for the termination, then I am afraid my business managers and I will have to sit down and do some hard thinking about how we spend our money. Regrettably, such budgetary considerations could lead to financial hardship for your organization."

"You're threatening to cut off our support, then, if I don't have Ilse killed."

"Nothing so barbaric as that," Churatov assured him. "A job needs doing, and we would like to know that it will be taken care of with the speed and efficiency we have come to expect. I urge you to be reasonable, my friend. Is doing what I ask so terrible? I think not. It is for the best. If you look to your heart, I believe you will see my solution to the problem is one Fräulein Stern would agree with. What do you say?"

"That you and your so-called business managers are all despicable bastards," Heisler answered. "Nevertheless, it shall be as you insist. I will arrange for one of my people to visit Ilse at the hospital."

"Excellent," Churatov said. "I knew you would not let us down."

15

Gregor Churatov ended his conversation with Heisler with mixed feelings. On the one hand he was amused by the Rote-Abend leader's sudden, yet brief, fling at independence in staging the city-center strike. Heisler had actually thought he could step out of line with impunity. Ridiculous. For all the terrorists' tough talk and violent schemes for saving the world from itself, Churatov had never come across a terrorist willing to put his ideals ahead of his bank balance.

Gunther Heisler was no exception. The man was a jellyfish, no backbone at all. He was precisely the kind of man the Soviet Union relied upon to foster terrorism throughout the globe.

Churatov shrugged off his amusement at Heisler's antics; when he thought about the problems to be faced before the weekend was over, he felt anything but amusement. With the scheduled trade of Karl Hahn for Josef Roetz coming down to the wire, the last thing Churatov needed right now was for Rote Abend to deliver an orphan of problems to his doorstep. And if Heisler and his followers were butting heads against the forces Churatov suspected they were, then Rote Abend's situation was sure to get worse before it got better.

The mysterious one-armed man Heisler had mentioned was the key to Churatov's concern. Unless Churatov was mistaken, the man with the hook and his friends were the same individuals responsible for the collapse of several KGB-sponsored operations in the past, including one disastrous venture that had claimed the lives of more than two hundred Soviet commandos.

If Churatov was correct about what the presence of the one-armed man in Bonn represented, then Heisler had his work cut out for him. Rote Abend would need every member it could lay its hands on, and even that was hardly a guarantee that Heisler's terrorists would be victorious in the end. And maybe in the long run, Churatov reflected, that wouldn't be so bad.

Funding Rote-Abend activities had served the Kremlin's interests well, but perhaps the time had come to close the chapter on Gunther Heisler and his fanatics. What better way could there be to accomplish that than to let someone else do Churatov's job for him? As long as the trail of bloodshed stayed well away from Churatov and the proposed prisoner exchange, then he had nothing to fear.

Rote Abend could serve as a buffer to any potential threats or danger until every last terrorist was dead. In which case Churatov would merely go shopping for another group looking for a handout. Outfits like Heisler's were very common.

Churatov looked at his watch and decided it was time to check on his guest. Hahn was an enigma. Nothing about being held prisoner with his life on the line seemed to bother the man, making Hahn one of three things: very stupid, very brave or a very good actor. Churatov could not decide which.

On the occasions when Churatov had spoken to him, Hahn never pressed him for more information than he was willing to divulge. The West-German operative's blasé attitude was frustrating. Even the slightest trace of fear in the man would have been welcome. Fear was an emotion Churatov could deal with; it could be cultivated, exploited. But not when the victim showed no fear at all.

An unsettling thought occurred to Churatov as he crossed to another room and ordered two of his men to accompany him downstairs to Hahn's cell. Did Rote Abend's recent rash of strategic blunders and misfortune have anything to do with their involvement in the capture of Hahn on Churatov's instructions? Or was it only a coincidence? Perhaps the BND agent could be persuaded or tricked into shedding some light on the matter.

Churatov and his escorts reached the door to Hahn's basement room, and Churatov threw the wall switch to turn on the lights inside. He nodded and one of his men unlocked the door and pulled it open, then stepped aside for Churatov to enter. Both armed guards remained outside as the Russian pulled the door closed behind him.

"Good afternoon," he said to Hahn, who was sitting on his mattress on the floor, his back propped against the wall. "Your lunch was satisfactory?"

"Delicious," Hahn replied. "Preparing shoe leather so that it resembles roast beef is quite an achievement. You must give me the recipe."

"I apologize for the poor quality of your meals," the Russian said. "If we were in my country..."

"The food would be the same, but we would have to wait in long lines to get it."

Churatov flashed a counterfeit smile. "I shall try to remember that joke for future reference. But—" he rubbed his hands together "—I have not come to hear your critique of the food. The time when you will be exchanged for Josef Roetz is fast approaching. Up till now I had every expectation that the proposed exchange would be carried out smoothly. Representatives of your government, in fact, gave me every assurance that the trade would be made without malice on their part. Now, it appears, they were less than honest with me. We have hit a snag."

Hahn stared blankly ahead, half expecting Churatov to tell him that Josef Roetz was dead, and that therefore there was no reason to keep Hahn alive. "Oh?" Hahn kept his tone level. "A snag?"

"That's right," Churatov answered. "Ever since Gunther Heisler delivered you to me, he and his Rote-Abend comrades have had nothing but trouble. Many of Heisler's people, in fact, have been killed."

"How unfortunate," Hahn said, relieved that Churatov was apparently still unaware that Josef Roetz was dead. "And you suspect my government's security forces are behind Heisler's problems?"

"I didn't say that," Churatov corrected. "I only said Heisler's comrades are being systematically eliminated, and whoever is behind the repeated attacks is not doing *you* any favor. If these unwarranted assaults continue, I may be forced to conclude that the proposed prisoner exchange is too dangerous.

"If the exchange is canceled for any reason, well, let me say it would prove extremely unhealthy for you. That is why it is important for both of us that I determine who is challenging Rote Abend. If any persons other than our government's security personnel are out to write Rote Abend's epitaph, then I need to know who they are."

"Don't misunderstand," Hahn answered. "Of course I am anxious for the trade for Herr Roetz to go through. But unless you are more specific, how can I possibly know who is clashing with Gunther Heisler and his friends? You are asking me to draw you a picture, and yet you provide neither pencil nor paper. Unless you are prepared to offer more specific details, then there is nothing I can tell you."

"Very well." Churatov shrugged in apparent acceptance. "I know little more, but I will tell you this. The leader of the men who have been so adept at sending Heisler's comrades to their graves is reported to have only one arm."

"Well!" Hahn exclaimed, doing his best to contain his excitement. "There you have it!"

"Excellent. You know of this one-armed marauder?"

"No," Hahn glibly lied. "But the fact that he has one arm tells me he has nothing to do with any of the security organizations of my country. The physical requirements are too stringent to permit anyone with such a handicap to join. My line of work is no place for a one-armed man."

Churatov frowned. "Somebody should tell him that."

16

"Bloody fine vacation this has turned out to be."

"Save it," Manning said. "We're in enough hot water as it is."

"I still haven't gone to see where Beethoven was born," James complained.

Manning groaned. "Not you, too."

"What do you think is taking so long?" Encizo wondered.

"They're probably having trouble deciding between hanging and a firing squad," Manning guessed. "I really regret getting Dieter mixed up in all of this."

"I'm certain Herr Beck will weather the storm thrown at him by his superiors," Katz said. "How the five of us fare, on the other hand, is another story."

For the past two hours, Phoenix Force had been gathering dust and cooling their heels in a maximum security holding tank at Bonn's BKA headquarters. Their weapons had been confiscated by the Bundeskriminalamt, as had the various documents of identification they had carried at the time of their arrest.

The solid steel door of the holding tank buzzed, then opened to admit a couple of unsmiling BKA agents, armed with H&K MP-5 submachine guns.

"Kommen," one of the two BKA men ordered.

"And about time, too," McCarter observed. "Whatever happened to hospitality? We're famished."

"Somehow I don't think they're here to take us to lunch," Encizo said.

"Schnell!" the second BKA operative directed and he and his partner ushered Phoenix Force from the room at gunpoint.

Three minutes, two hallways and one flight of stairs later, the Stony-Man crew reached their destination— the office of Polizeioberrat Gerald Mader, Chief Superintendent of the BKA. Mader, his rank designated by a single gold star worn on the epaulettes of his coat, was a stocky middle-aged man with a round face and coarse black hair. His eyes looked like a pair of tiny marbles. His nose appeared squashed, as though it had been dropped against his face from a great height.

Mader remained seated at his desk as the men of Phoenix Force were escorted into the office and lined up facing the superintendent. Dieter Beck stood at attention on Mader's left. It was evident from Beck's expression that the time he had spent with Mader had not been pleasant.

Mader instructed the two armed guards to remain outside his office door, then waited for them to obey his command before speaking to the prisoners.

"You men have much to answer for," Mader informed them in heavily accented English. "I scarcely know where to begin. You have been in this country less than twenty-four hours, and have already engaged in a full-scale gun battle on the streets of the city. You have personally contributed to the deaths of more than two dozen West-German citizens."

"Those citizens happened to be Rote-Abend terrorists, who lost their lives trying to kill us," Katz returned.

"Ah," Mader said sighing. "You are claiming self-defense, then?"

"If we have to," the Israeli told him.

"We shall see," Mader said. "Tell me, why did the five of you come to Bonn?"

Gary Manning supplied the answer. "To help a friend of ours who is in trouble."

"And the friend's name?"

"Karl Hahn," Calvin James stated. "Does the name ring a bell?"

"*Ja*, the name is not unfamiliar to me. How is it that you know of him?"

"How we happen to know Karl Hahn is unimportant," Katz said. "What does matter is that Hahn was captured during an assault on a Rote-Abend base in which the two BfV agents with him were murdered.

We know that Hahn is being held prisoner, and that his captors have demanded that a Communist spy named Josef Roetz be released from Stammheim Prison in exchange for Hahn. Unfortunately for Hahn, Josef Roetz died earlier in the week from a self-inflicted wound to the throat. In short, Hahn is still for sale, but now your government has nothing to buy him with.''

"And so you decided to take it upon yourselves to help Karl Hahn on your own?"

"Somebody had to do it." McCarter's response was swift. "From what we were able to find out from our end, most of your lot were tackling the problem sitting on their asses. That may be fine from where you're parked, but come Monday morning when Josef Roetz fails to sing and dance for his friends, then Karl Hahn's a goner."

"Who authorized this rescue mission of yours?" Mader wanted to know.

"No one within the Federal Republic, if that's what you mean," Katzenelenbogen said. "We acted independently."

"And proceeded, with Dieter Beck's willing assistance, to go about killing individuals you claim threatened your lives." Mader shook his head. "Your personal vendetta has been most disruptive. We do not condone vigilante justice. Unlike some countries where such wanton acts are tolerated, all citizens of the Federal Republic of Germany are protected by the

Grundgesetz, the Basic Law; and for each of the individuals your men killed, that Basic Law was violated."

"And where was the Basic Law's protection when Rote Abend turned Bonn's Innenstadt into an outdoor shooting gallery this morning?" Rafael Encizo questioned. "Four policemen were murdered, and the death toll of innocent bystanders is still climbing. If not for our intervention, the terrorists would have killed many more people, and could conceivably have escaped until the next time they decided to flex their muscles."

"Another thing," James added. "I'm referring to your ridiculous implication that the Rote-Abend creeps we met up with didn't really try to kill us. You'll pardon my French, Herr Mader, but that's a load of bullshit, and you know it. Basic Law or not, every one of those bastards got what they deserved."

"That more or less sums up Herr Beck's assessment of the situation," Mader confessed in an annoyed tone.

"Then the BKA should open its ears and start listening," Katz advised. "And quit trying to measure Rote Abend for halos. They're a pack of vicious killers who have given up the privilege of living in a society that values the safety of its citizens."

"The BKA cannot condone murder," Mader said.

"What about the weapons we uncovered at the factory last night?" McCarter countered. "What do you think Rote Abend planned to do with all that gear? Serve it for tea with scones and cucumber sandwiches?'' The cockney laughed. ''Hard cheese on that one, governor. If it hadn't been for us stepping in when we did, the terrorists would have had all that weaponry packed off and hidden somewhere else.''

''Your role in our acquisition of Rote Abend's cache of weapons has not been overlooked,'' Mader acknowledged. ''Quite frankly, it is all that is keeping me from throwing the five of you in prison right now and forgetting where I put the key. Also in your favor are the words I have shared with Beck here. He is a good man and I usually respect his judgment, although this time I feel he has overstepped the boundaries of discretion. Nevertheless, I have decided to be lenient.

''First, though,'' Mader backtracked, ''you must tell me how it is you know about Karl Hahn's predicament, not to mention Josef Roetz's suicide. Herr Beck was hopelessly vague at explaining these things to me.''

''That is because Dieter doesn't know any more about us than you do,'' Manning offered.

''And yet Herr Beck willingly aided you in your quest to rescue Hahn.''

''Dieter and I knew each other from when we were with the GSG-9,'' the Canadian revealed. ''But I'm afraid you're out of luck if you're shooting for more information.''

"You were saying something about leniency," reminded Katz.

"Yes," Mader said. "Rather than throw you in prison I am giving you until midnight tonight to leave this country on your own. I have been assured by Herr Beck that you will comply with this order, and I tell you honestly that it will signal the end of his career if you do not.

"Your passport and other forms of identification will be returned to you upon your departure. Your confiscated weapons, however, will remain our property. Once you have left Bonn, we expect never to see you here again. Understood?"

"What about Karl Hahn?" Manning asked.

"Hahn is no longer your concern," Mader replied. "Now, do you agree to my terms or not?"

"We agree," Katz said reluctantly. "We'll be out of here by midnight."

"Good," Mader said. "Oh, just one more thing. It concerns the Maserati that was taken from the Innenstadt. The mayor's wife reported it stolen. Which of you men took it?"

McCarter coughed and said to his friends, "Why don't you wait for me outside?"

17

The doctor was sorry, but he did not have time to answer the question asked by the patient in the wheelchair. Later, perhaps, but not right now. The doctor had an emergency on his hands that could not wait.

He turned away from the patient and hurried briskly down the hospital corridor to where three nurses were about to enter an elevator. The doctor followed them inside and the elevator doors closed. The three nurses smiled at the doctor, but he was staring at his watch and did not smile back. Then the elevator stopped at the second floor and the nurses got off. But not the doctor. His destination was one floor above.

Third-floor traffic was light as the doctor emerged from the elevator and turned right. His pulse quickened, and his upper lip was moist. His throat felt sandpaper dry. Less than a minute to go.

Pushing through a swinging door, the doctor found himself in a long narrow hallway lined on either side with doors to private rooms. Three armed men stood guard outside the door at the end of the corridor, and they watched the doctor warily as he approached.

Now the doctor did smile. His smile was warm and friendly and full of promise, just the kind to put the guards' minds at ease.

"Good evening, Doctor," one of the armed men greeted him. "How may we help you?"

"I just came by to tell you that we will soon be moving our important guest."

"Oh?" The guard traded looks with his colleagues. "That's news to us. Why haven't we been told?"

"I'm sure you will be, quite soon," the doctor said. "We are already preparing her new room and should be taking her there within the hour."

"Why move her?" asked the second guard suspiciously. "What's wrong with this room?"

"Nothing at all," the doctor replied, "but the new room will be more isolated and easier for you to protect."

"We're not complaining," said guard number three. "She's fine right where she is."

"That may be, but she's still going to..." The doctor stopped as the electronic pager clipped to the breast pocket of the shirt beneath his coat began to beep. "Excuse me," he apologized, reaching inside his white lab coat to switch off the beeper. "It must be an emergency."

The noise from the beeper died, and so did the three armed guards, thanks to the silencer-equipped Beretta the doctor pulled from his coat. One, two, three, and it was over, each of the guards spilling to the floor with a bullet to the brain.

The doctor stepped over the bodies and entered the room the dead men had been guarding. The room was sparsely furnished with just a bed, a nightstand and a chair for visitors.

On the bed lay Ilse Stern, with tubes feeding fluids into and out of her body, and wired to a machine nearby that monitored her vital signs. As the doctor crossed the room to her bedside, the woman stirred and her eyelids fluttered open.

"Gunther sends his love."

"Since when are you a doctor?" she asked, her voice weak.

"I'm whatever I have to be. Do you hurt?"

"No."

"Good. You know why I have come?"

"I knew Gunther had to send someone. I am glad it was you."

"So am I. Please now, shut your eyes. I have so little time."

"Tell Gunther I do not blame him. Will you?"

"Yes. Please."

Ilse Stern shut her eyes, then the doctor closed them forever.

GUNTHER HEISLER SAT ALONE in the darkness of his converted basement, his anger boiling within him. Ilse was dead. He had ordered her death and now she was gone. Her execution was the first Rote-Abend operation in two days not to be ruined by interference from the one-armed man and his friends.

Success had never tasted so bitter.

Heisler clenched his fists until his fingernails dug into his palms. Ilse's death had accomplished two things: first, the authorities had been prevented from using her to reach Rote Abend, and second, the financial support from Churatov that Rote Abend depended upon for survival would continue uninterrupted. Heisler needed to remember these things, to justify Ilse's death and his role in causing it.

The negative results of Ilse's death were many. As one of Rote Abend's few female members she had served as a role model for other women recruits to answer the call to duty. Ilse's astute insights and observations had often meant the difference between the success or failure of a mission. Finally, Heisler recalled with a groan, Ilse was a tigress in bed. There was no doubt about it—her loss would be felt for years to come.

And all because that one-armed bastard had targeted Rote Abend for extinction. Heisler had no idea where the man and his equally troublesome friends had come from, but logic dictated that such a highly efficient team of killers could not go about their business openly without a nod of approval from the West-

German government. So be it. They would all be made
to pay.

At dawn on Monday the exchange of prisoners
would be carried out as planned. Gregor Churatov
would have his precious Josef Roetz, and Karl
Hahn would be returned to the BND. And after the
trade was completed, Rote Abend would present to the
citizens of Bonn a special gift. An unexpected surprise. A crash course in dying.

Heisler smiled, resolving to put his gloomy mood
aside and concentrate on positive thinking and action. There was much to be done. First he would see
to it that Ilse's death was avenged. He had called for
Rote Abend's reserve forces to join him in Bonn, and
the response to his summons had been much faster and
more enthusiastic than he had expected.

Six newcomers had already arrived and were upstairs now, conferring with their local comrades and
eagerly anticipating the revenge they would exact upon
their unsuspecting foes. And the six were just the
trickle before the flood. By midnight Heisler expected
to again be able to fill the seats of his meeting room
with an army of Rote-Abend followers. *His* followers. All of them anxiously awaiting his instructions on
their next operation.

Instructions Heisler was eager to give. The West-
German government had aided Rote Abend's enemies and must not escape unpunished. A show of
strength and solidarity was required, a bold slap in the

face of authority. Heisler knew that the best way to disrupt a political machine was to embarrass the hell out of it.

At the same time, by means of secrets whispered in the proper ears, Rote Abend would never again be threatened by the one-armed man and his friends.

18

From his pinched mouth and the watering of his marble eyes Chief Superintendent Gerald Mader could have been sitting on a nest of fire ants. His brow was sweaty, and he scowled now as he waited for the men of Phoenix Force, along with Dieter Beck, to file into his office once again and take up their position in front of his desk. When his aide had left the room, Mader shifted uncomfortably in his seat and loudly cleared his throat.

"I have just had my ass chewed off by the Polizeipräsident of the BKA," Mader told them honestly. "This has not been a good day."

"In another couple of hours we would have been out of the country," Yakov Katzenelenbogen said. "Is this your way of telling us we're in more trouble than we were before?"

"I wish it were that simple," Mader muttered. "But no, you are not in more trouble. Quite the opposite. Now I am the one dancing in the fire."

"You?" Katz raised his eyebrow. "But why?"

"I am coming to that," Mader answered, clearing his throat again, then taking a drink of water. "Since we spoke a short time ago, events have occurred that we feel seriously jeopardize our chances of rescuing Karl Hahn. It was our hope that Ilse Stern, the Rote-Abend terrorist you captured earlier today, could be persuaded to reveal Herr Hahn's whereabouts to us in time to save his life."

"And now?" Gary Manning inquired.

"Now whatever the woman could have told us will never be known. Ilse Stern is dead."

"She was in pretty bad shape when they hauled her away in the ambulance," James said. "What happened? Did she die of her injuries? Did she pull herself together enough to commit suicide?"

"Had either of those things happened, it would have been unfortunate, but the truth is even worse. Ilse Stern was murdered. Executed by one of her own people."

"What about our men who were guarding her?" asked Beck.

"The same," Mader replied. "All three were found dead outside the Stern woman's room immediately before her body was discovered inside."

"Did anyone see anything?" Encizo asked.

"Some nurses remember riding in an elevator with a doctor they'd never seen before, but beyond that, nothing. We have their descriptions of the suspect, but that may not lead to anything useful."

"That sums up this whole conversation, as far as we're concerned," an impatient McCarter interrupted. "Ilse Stern is dead. So are three of your men, and your governor's cheesed off about it. What's that got to do with me and my friends?"

"I have been instructed," Mader stated stiffly, "to retract your order of expulsion from the Federal Republic of Germany and to officially extend to you the complete cooperation and assistance of this department so that the matter of Karl Hahn's abduction can be resolved as soon as possible."

Calvin James frowned. "Let me translate that. The BKA wants to help *us* now?"

Mader nodded.

"Why the change of heart?" Manning asked. "The last time we were in your office you treated us not much better than the dirt under your fingernails."

"My opinion of you has not changed," Mader snapped. "I still believe the five of you are extremely dangerous men, and that you must be crazy, besides, to think you could come to Bonn, uninvited, to wage this war of yours with the Rote-Abend butchers. Unfortunately my personal feelings have no bearing on the distasteful duty I have been ordered to perform. The only reason I am putting the services of the BKA at your disposal is that I have been ordered to do so."

"How touching," James said. "We'll remember your vote of confidence the next time Rote Abend uses us for target practice."

"Then consider this also," Mader added. "Before he did this impressive turnaround, Polizeipräsident Lichter recommended that I throw you in prison. He has even less tolerance for your kind than I have. Yet now he is your best friend in Bonn. Remarkable. He does not like our helping you any more than I do, but obviously someone higher in the chain of command disagrees. And knowing that tells me there is much more to you five men than meets the eye. You obviously have friends in very high places."

"So much for yesterday's news," McCarter said. "When do we get our gear back?"

"How soon would you like it?"

"Ten minutes ago," the cockney told Mader.

The BKA's chief superintendent spoke into an intercom, requesting that the Stony-Man crew's weapons be delivered to his office at once.

"There," Mader said. "How else may the BKA be of service?"

"Two ways," Katzenelenbogen replied. "First, do you understand the phrase 'keep your ear to the ground'?"

"You mean like in the American Western movies where the Indian scout would press his ear to the earth and listen for the sound of horses?" Mader asked.

"Correct," the Israeli commando said. "We will do everything we can to find Karl Hahn. In the meantime, I would like you to put all available BKA personnel on the streets of Bonn and have them become our eyes and ears. At this point we cannot afford to overlook anything.

"Keep whatever information your people are able to dig up. Don't censor any of it, and discard nothing even if it seems irrelevant. Let me be the one to decide if it's any use to us or not. I'm assuming you'll be here for the rest of the night, so you can expect a call from me every hour on the hour. Eventually, if things work out, we'll be able to lock horns with Rote Abend again. That's when I'll need you and your BKA to do the second thing I want."

"And what is that?" Mader asked.

Katz answered firmly, "Stay out of our way."

19

Phoenix Force and Dieter Beck had been waiting in the parking lot outside Stimson Memorial Chapel for more than two hours, and David McCarter was beginning to wish he had something more to occupy his time than the incessant pounding of raindrops on the roof of the minibus they were sitting in.

"I'm bored," McCarter said.

"Have another can of Coke," Manning suggested. "That should take care of thirty seconds."

"I don't dare," McCarter said. "Another sip and I'll have to take a leak for sure."

"Shit," James grumbled. "Are they going to hit the church or what?"

"We can't be sure that the information the BKA uncovered about a strike against the chapel is valid," Dieter Beck replied. Manning's friend from the BKA checked his watch. "Anyway, it's almost twelve o'clock. The church service will end soon."

"At which time almost everyone attending will join us here in the parking lot," Encizo said.

"From what we witnessed yesterday in the Innenstadt," Katz added, "that would be an ideal moment for Rote Abend to strike. Gunning down helpless individuals seems to be irresistible to these animals."

"Yeah, well, just let the bastards give us the pleasure of their company," McCarter said. "I've got a few games of my own."

Stimson Memorial Chapel was in an American community in Plittersdorf, a suburb of Bonn–Bad Godesberg, on the banks of the Rhine, about five kilometers from the American Embassy.

The American Embassy in Bonn, employing more than three hundred fifty Americans and close to three hundred sixty foreign nationals, represented one of the largest United States missions overseas. Plittersdorf's home-away-from-home atmosphere provided numerous amenities, including a theater, commissary, service station, twelve-grade elementary and secondary school, community center, and church, the Stimson Memorial Chapel, where a Catholic priest and a Protestant minister served the community's spiritual needs.

"Yo," James called softly. "It looks like the BKA info was legit."

A Volkswagen van pulled off the street fronting the chapel and slowly entered the parking lot next to the church. It started up the row of vehicles where Phoenix Force had parked their minibus, but turned into an empty space closer to the road.

The driver of the van shut off the engine, freezing the windshield wipers in midsweep. Although the van's side windows were steamy, the outlines of four or more passengers could be seen. None of the passengers left the vehicle.

"What do you think?" Encizo asked.

"Three minutes before twelve," Beck announced.

"It's for damn sure they're not here for their weekly dose of religion," Manning decided, easing his Eagle .357 from its holster.

"Bloody right," agreed McCarter, feeling better now that their wait appeared to be over. "This is the last service at the chapel until seven tonight." He jerked his thumb in the direction of the van. "Unless these geezers have shown up awfully early for vespers, then I'd say they've popped round just now for a bit of nasty business."

A moment later the van's side door slid open and the first of the Volkswagen's passengers, a man in his late twenties, hopped out into the rain. His poorly concealed Uzi submachine gun stood out like a grotesque extension of his right arm. He moved aside to enable another of the van's armed passengers to join him.

"Time to go," Katz said.

Then the Israeli and his Stony-Man teammates, along with Dieter Beck, rushed from the minibus to intercept the Rote-Abend terrorists before they could launch their strike against the American churchgoers about to leave the chapel. Keeping low to avoid being seen, the six counterterrorists approached their enemies in pairs.

Katzenelenbogen and James went up the row of cars their minibus was parked in, while McCarter and Encizo circled around to reach the VW van from the next aisle over. Gary Manning and his friend from the BKA zigzagged between two rows as they moved toward the killers' vehicle.

There were now five gunmen gathered around the van, and another was in the process of getting out, when the first terrorist motioned for the others to follow, then led the way across the parking lot to the doors of the chapel. The assassin carrying the Uzi was halfway across the row closest to the church, when he glanced to the right...and saw McCarter and Encizo.

The killer's eyes went wide and he opened his mouth to warn his comrades, simultaneously swinging his Uzi around to mow down the Phoenix-Force pair. Encizo beat him to it with a hot salvo of MP-5 destruction. The 9 mm rounds tore along the terrorist's chest in a diagonal line. His lifeless body back flipped awkwardly and came to rest on the rain-slick pavement of the parking lot.

Stunned by the unexpected turn of events, all but one of the five remaining killers froze. The exception was the thug who had been walking behind the slain Uzi owner.

Dropping to his hands and knees, the terrorist inched forward until he guessed he could peek safely around the rear bumper of a parked car in search of the unseen shooter who had just polished off his friend. The killer peered around the bumper, and a stream of Ingram persuaders from McCarter's MAC-10 blipped the side of his head, sending him into a universe of darkness.

The next Rote-Abend gunman in line reacted to the second killer's passing by turning right around and trying to regain the dubious refuge of the Volkswagen. Many obstacles stood in his way, including his three surviving comrades, who were frantically trying to achieve the same goal. The barrier that stopped the gunman cold was a single shot from Gary Manning's Eagle, which burned a hot hole through the gunman's belly. Doubling over in agony, the wounded killer spilled to the ground and began to bleed to death.

Spotting Manning as he put his .357 to work, the three Rote-Abend terrorists still on their feet quickly targeted the Canadian for instant oblivion. He barely had time to dive below the oncoming rush of firepower before the air over his head and Beck's was transformed into a curtain of death.

On his left side on the pavement, Dieter Beck took aim with his Heckler and Koch machine pistol and unleashed a barrage of bullets that passed beneath the parked cars between him and the Rote-Abend trio. For one of the terrorists, Beck's below-the-belt attack was the beginning of the end.

Engulfed in molten pain, the killer shrieked as he realized the jagged red and white splinters protruding through his trousers were the shattered remnants of his leg bones. His destroyed tibia and fibula were unable to support his weight, and the screaming gunman collapsed into the path of a fresh wave of Beck's H&K rounds. The screams and the terrorist making them died together.

The last two Rote-Abend killers were beginning to think they might reach their van unscathed, when Katz and James appeared from out of nowhere on their left and popped their bubble of hope. The first of the two terrorists blew away the taillights of the car next to the Stony-Man pair, missing them by a wide margin.

Katz's Uzi and James's M-76 sang in unison, sweeping over the killers and drowning their sorrows in a flash of heat and light. The gunman who had shot out the taillights dropped his submachine gun and sprawled over the hood of a BMW coupe. At the same time the last terrorist slammed against the VW van and slid to the ground, leaving a trail of blood in his wake, which the rain soon washed away.

Certain now that the last of the gunmen from the van was dead, Katz called out that the coast was clear.

"Six up, six down," Dieter Beck said as he and Manning climbed to their feet. "I may be soaked to the skin, my clothes are ruined and I will probably develop a terrible head cold, but I don't care. We got all the terrorist trash before a single one of the churchgoers could be harmed. Once again, Gary, you and your remarkable friends have saved the day.''

"Thanks, Dieter," Manning said, "but we all claim first prize, and that includes you."

The doors to Stimson Memorial Chapel slowly opened and a sea of curious faces stared cautiously toward the parking lot, prompting Beck to comment to Manning, "I'll return in a minute. It's important that the congregation be reassured that they have nothing to fear."

Beck turned and walked toward the church, leaving Manning to join his Phoenix-Force teammates. Although it was still raining, the worst of the morning's downpour appeared to be over, having slackened to a misty drizzle.

Manning reached the VW van and said to Katz, "Dieter's gone to calm down the people in the church."

"Good," Katz said. "As soon as he's finished I'll remind him to radio Chief Superintendent Mader at BKA headquarters so that Mader can get some police out here."

"Speaking of Mader," Encizo said, "I've been wondering just why we didn't get our cans kicked out of the country after all."

"Mader mentioned that someone high up in the chain of command put in a good word for us,"

McCarter replied. "Maybe Hal's behind our change of luck."

"It's certainly possible," Katz said. "Mader made no secret of the fact that both he and his boss wanted to deport us. Getting them to reverse their decision had to take muscle. If Hal isn't the one responsible, then I can't imagine who is."

"I don't know about the rest of you guys," Manning said, "but I'm kind of surprised that the garbage from this van was all Rote Abend sent."

Encizo nodded. "Me, too. From what Beck's BKA pals were able to uncover, I would have expected Rote Abend to send out a much larger strike force. Not that I'm complaining."

"We've been cleaning Rote Abend's house since we came to Bonn," James pointed out. "Perhaps we've put a bigger dent in their membership than we realize. These six might be the last of the lot, the bottom of the barrel."

"Either that or Rote Abend didn't think extra guns would be necessary," McCarter suggested. "Not when all they were planning was gunning down a bunch of helpless people coming out of church."

Manning smiled. "Didn't turn out that way, though, did it?"

"It makes a difference when the intended victims can shoot back," Katz said.

"Sure as hell mattered to these six yobbos," McCarter decided, then added to James, "Right, mate?"

But when James, who stood facing the street, opened his mouth to reply, all that came out was, "Holy shit!"

20

The three Rote-Abend vehicles converged on the area fronting Stimson Memorial Chapel with a roar of engines and squeal of tires. The doors to the two Mercedes-Benz sedans and the Volvo diesel station wagon slammed open in unison. Sixteen armed terrorists leaped from the cars.

Reacting to Rote Abend's attack with the speed and precision that ranked them among the world's foremost counterterrorists, the Stony-Man crew quickly fanned out to confront their murderous adversaries. Before Katz, Manning, McCarter and Encizo reached the vantage points they were making for, the Smith and Wesson SMG James was carrying set the pace for the fight to follow.

James positioned himself behind a parked car and opened fire. The black Phoenix warrior's unerring aim with his M-76 fed two Rote-Abend killers a lead sandwich that went straight to their guts.

The dumbstruck duo stopped dead as their bellies sprouted red. They lost their weapons, doubled over and fell forward, writing on the pavement like earthworms on hooks.

James saw his targets go down before dropping below the side of the car he was using for cover. A heartbeat later the windows above his head were perforated with holes by a flurry of Rote-Abend rounds. James shielded his eyes from the shower of spraying glass, waiting for the hellish storm to pass. When it finally did, he reloaded. The fresh magazine would give him thirty more opportunities to take out the opposition.

Dieter Beck was standing at the entrance to the church when the new wave of enemy Rote-Abend assassins unexpectedly appeared. He shouted in alarm and began shoving as many churchgoers as he could back into the building. The BKA agent's efforts were only partially successful, for several onlookers stayed, staring transfixed at the drama unfolding just beyond the church.

Then a rifle-launched grenade exploded against the chapel's main doors. Three men at the doors died instantly, absorbing the brunt of the blast in a wall of flying shrapnel and splintered wood. Ironically, the buffer of their mutilated bodies helped save the lives of many of those Beck was herding farther into the church. Amid their screams of terror, Beck managed to get most of the frightened congregation between the pews and onto the floor near the pulpit before a second grenade followed the first. Beck yelled for everyone to remain where they were until he returned, then, toting his H&K MP-5, he ran out a door behind the altar, which would lead him to an exit at the opposite end of the church from the beleaguered front doors.

The clamor of the second explosion rang through the air as David McCarter caught sight of the terrorist wielding the FN/FAL rifle-grenade combo. He was preparing to launch grenade number three.

"Not this time, sunshine," the Londoner muttered.

McCarter brought up his mighty MAC-10 and a three-round burst reduced the distracted rifleman's head to a fountain of sticky despair. The killer's FAL slipped from his fingers and he crumpled in a bloody heap. McCarter withdrew at once to another location before any Rote-Abend opponents could zero in on him.

Three enterprising assassins had rushed around to the far end of the chapel's parking lot, hoping to sneak up on Phoenix Force from behind. Confident their tactic would spell doom for their foes, the anxious killers were single-filing it from one car to the next, when they happened to dart between the two automobiles where Rafael Encizo had set up shop.

The Cuban commando took the three terrorists by surprise, but that wasn't the only shock they got. Peppered with a swarm of 9 mm rounds from Encizo's MP-5 machine pistol that swept across them from left to right, the killers took the road to early retirement in a flash of burning pain.

One terrorist clocked out when a pair of bullets mangled his intestines, while the other two hoodlums wheezed their last breaths through lungs that looked like bloody Swiss cheese. Together the three killers toppled to the wet cement as if a rug had been pulled from beneath their feet.

The deaths of the terrorists Encizo had eliminated did not go unnoticed. No sooner had the Cuban put the trio out of action than two more Rote-Abend gunmen began closing in on him from opposite directions. Encizo did not see them. Yakov Katzenelenbogen did.

Kneeling alongside an American Ford Thunderbird, the Israeli colonel calculated which of the two posed the greater danger to Encizo, and eradicated that threat with his Uzi. Katz's bullets found their intended target and stitched a destructive path along the killer's rib cage. The terrorist twisted in agony and stretched his arms overhead, shaking his fingers at the gray clouds of the stormy afternoon sky. A final Uzi round found the crown of his skull and the killer's corpse collapsed in a heap.

Katz directed his Uzi to where he had last seen the second Rote-Abend gunman, but the killer was nowhere in sight. The problem of the elusive assassin's whereabouts had to be put on the back burner, however, as a barrage of enemy bullets thudded into the body of the T-Bird. Katz flattened himself on the wet pavement.

The second killer Katz had been gunning for had fallen to his knees when he saw his comrade-in-arms succumb to the Israeli's Uzi. Determined to find out where the shots that killed his partner had come from, he decided to search under the parked cars for his enemy.

After crawling on hands and knees to a likely place to begin looking, the killer stopped and lowered his face close to the pavement. He let his eyes roam across the parking lot until, four cars along the row of parked automobiles, he found an unfamiliar face staring back at him. Incredible, he thought. The person the face belonged to had some kind of gun in his hand, and it was pointing straight at . . .

Gary Manning fired two head shots with his Eagle .357, and the powerful Magnum rounds dispatched the curious Rote-Abend terrorist. Manning made sure his target was dead, then moved farther down the line of parked cars to search for more killers.

DIETER BECK JUMPED BACK as the doorknob he had just grabbed was pulled from his hand. The door at the rear of Stimson Memorial Chapel opened and two terrorists, one a woman with stringy brown hair hanging over her shoulders, tried to run inside. What stopped them was Beck's quick thinking and the stream of hot lead from the BKA man's Heckler and Koch.

Eager to be the first of her comrades to kill some of the helpless people she knew were within the church, the Rote-Abend female put the skids on her plans as she rushed face to face with Beck. Wearing an expression of pure hatred, she attempted to fire her submachine gun, but Beck beat her to the punch. Her SMG went flying and her lips pouted in a kiss as her face struck the floor.

Next, the terrorist providing backup for the woman felt MP-5 bullets tear into his chest. A wash of red splashed over his eyes. As the killer died his finger tightened reflexively on the trigger of his French MAS assault rifle. The lone .223 Remington round discharged from the MAS did not travel far.

Beck groaned as a searing brand of white-hot hurt ate through the deltoid muscle of his right shoulder. His fingers lost their grip on the MP-5, and his Heckler and Koch machine pistol slipped to his feet. His head swam, his knees buckled and the next thing he knew he was sitting on the floor with his back to the wall. He pressed the palm of his left hand to his wound. A moment later his hand fell limply again as his eyes rolled upward in their sockets and a veil of darkness put him to sleep.

Outside the church, the original Rote-Abend strike force had been reduced by more than half. With the odds no longer in their favor the five surviving Rote-

Abend terrorists came to the conclusion that retreat might be a good idea. Things were bad now, but they were bound to get worse. Police cars with sirens were closing in. In a matter of minutes all avenues out of Plittersdorf would be closed.

Calling for his fellow terrorists to join him, one of the gun-toting killers unleashed an indiscriminate spray of subgun fire at the twin rows of cars in the parking lot, a tactic designed to intimidate his opponents long enough for him to reach one of the Rote-Abend vehicles and drive away.

Concealed behind a Mitsubishi hatchback, David McCarter watched the terrorist wielding the SMG as he charged toward the Volvo station wagon he had arrived in. McCarter set aside his Ingram and reached for the Browning Hi-Power he carried in shoulder leather. The finest pistol marksman on the Phoenix-Force team carefully took aim with the autoloader and fired three quick shots.

The first of the Browning's 9 mm rounds connected with the terrorist's hip, while the next two shots played tag among the gunman's intestines. The killer shrieked, lost his submachine gun, then spun in a pirouette that landed him on his ass in a rain puddle. A fourth shot from the Hi-Power sped the already dying killer on his way.

If the rest of the terrorists still believed escape in their vehicles was possible, Rafael Encizo promptly dashed those hopes by shooting out the tires on all three Rote-Abend cars. The terrorists stopped as both the Mercedes and the Volvo settled onto metal rims, then the four split up to try to escape on foot. Two of the gunmen ran for the public park on the other side of the chapel. The second pair of killers about-faced and headed across the street toward the multi-story apartment buildings that housed U.S. embassy personnel.

Gary Manning jumped to his feet to chase the armed duo racing for the embassy housing complex, and was soon joined by a determined Encizo. The Canadian glanced at his Cuban companion and commented as they ran, "Our terrorist friends seem in a hurry."

"They have good reason to be," said Encizo.

THE TERRORIST PAIR charging for the nearby park were sure they would reach their goal. Inside the park they could either hide amid the trees and vegetation, or find a hostage to barter for their freedom. Either way they would survive the terrible conflict that had claimed the lives of all but a handful of their Rote-Abend friends.

"We are almost there," one gunman gasped as his legs struggled to maintain the torturous pace. "Almost to the park."

The killer's partner did not respond immediately, but chose that moment to look over his shoulder. What he saw did little to cheer him. Three men were chasing and gaining on them, and one of the pursuers was the one-armed man Gunther Heisler had warned them about.

"We are defeated," the second killer informed the first. "Even if we reach the park, hostage or no hostage, we will never leave there alive. We must make a stand and fight."

"Where? Here in the open? You are talking suicide!"

"Here or in the park...it makes no difference. Either way we are doomed. The best we can hope for is to take the cripple with us. Agreed?"

"Agreed," came the reluctant reply. "When?"

"On three."

Less than thirty meters separated the Phoenix-Force trio from their foes when the Rote-Abend pair unexpectedly halted, dug their heels into the water-soaked earth and whirled around with their submachine guns blazing. McCarter hit the dirt and rolled to his left. Katz and James dived to the right.

Unprepared for the evasive maneuver, the terrorist subgunners desperately worked to correct their aim, though they were undecided which of their enemy targets to shoot down first. By the time they had the answer, the question no longer mattered.

Coming out of his body roll with his Browning Hi-Power in hand and looking for blood, McCarter began firing as enemy slugs homed in on his position. The first shot went higher than the courageous East

Ender liked, but he still succeeded in drilling the terrorist closest to him through the throat.

A bright red stream gushed from the entry wound, and the gunshot killer thrashed his way into eternity, stopping just short of strangling himself as he tried to stem the torrent of blood from his ruptured throat. A follow-up shot from the Browning shattered his sternum, sending splinters of bone throughout his chest and abdomen.

Katz and James dispatched the other terrorist with a deadly hail of bullets. Chattering together the Israeli's Uzi and the American's M-76 made mincemeat of their adversary.

Hit from head to groin with enough lead to open a paperweight factory, the Rote-Abend killer hopped and danced as if his feet were on fire. Then his body was plunged into a pool of icy water and the flames were put out.

McCarter stood and said to Katz and James, "Two down and two to go."

"Yeah," James said wearily. "But who's keeping score?"

ENCIZO AND MANNING were scarcely thirty seconds behind the two Rote-Abend gunmen hurrying toward the apartment house. The building was divided into three sections of six apartments each, and each section had its own front steps and door.

Without looking back at their pursuers, the terrorists pushed their way through swinging doors and entered the left-hand section of the building. Steps to the immediate right climbed to the apartments overhead. A shorter staircase at the end of the foyer led to the basement. Through the glass doors Encizo and Manning saw one killer go upstairs, the other down.

"I'll take the high road," Manning volunteered, before Encizo could express a preference. Manning remembered well how Encizo nearly lost his life battling ODESSA forces in France, and had no desire for a repeat performance.

"And I'll take the low road," Encizo said.

As they opened the glass doors they could see the building's foyer was empty. Wishing each other good hunting, they entered the foyer and went their separate ways, Encizo silently descending to the basement, while Manning climbed after the footsteps he could hear retreating overhead.

In the basement a long narrow hallway ran the width of the building. Lining the corridor on either side, doors led to storage rooms, hobby rooms and servants' quarters. Light bulbs glowed at twenty-foot intervals along the hallway's ceiling.

The terrorist Encizo had followed to the basement was three-fourths of the way to the corridor's end, when Encizo entered the basement and shouted for his quarry to halt. The Red-Evening killer ignored the command and ran faster.

Encizo swore and chased after him, once more ordering the Rote-Abend gunman to halt. This time the Cuban's command was obeyed, but not as he'd intended.

Stopping abruptly, the gunman turned around and tried to unload all the bullets from his SMG at Encizo. Before the killer could carry out his aim though, the Cuban commando fired more than a dozen rocketing rounds from his H&K MP-5.

The startled terrorist felt pain explode in his body again and again. A volcano erupted inside his chest, and his stomach burned with the heat of a million suns. He squeezed the trigger of his submachine gun and killed a lone light bulb in the ceiling. He coughed and tasted blood, felt his knees begin to buckle, then flopped against a wall, painting it red as he slid to the floor.

Gary Manning made it to the landing on the building's first floor and kept on climbing. The terrorist he was chasing was in too much of a hurry to be quiet as he fled in panic to the floors above.

Manning's legs worked like pistons as he took the steps two and three at a time. He reached the second-story landing and paused as the sound of the fleeing terrorist's progress suddenly died. Manning listened, his heart pounding, the .357 Eagle clenched in his right fist. The Rote-Abend gunman had to be just overhead.

A faint squeaking came from the third floor above. A door handle being tested? Manning wondered. Then came a sound like a body slamming against a door. Manning raced up the next flight of stairs as a single gunshot echoed throughout the stairwell, followed by wood slapping against wood and a woman's shrill scream.

Manning hit the top of the landing as the screams grew louder and a man's voice swore in German. To the Canadian's left a lock had been blasted from a door. The door stood open. Another door slammed shut inside and the cries of terror were muffled into silence. The swearing continued.

Manning entered the apartment. From a short hallway he moved into a living-room dining area. Floor-to-ceiling windows opened onto a small balcony between a dining table and a pale green three-cushion divan. A coffee table in front of the couch was overturned. The hallway began again on the opposite side of the room, and it was there that the Rote-Abend terrorist was shouting in rage, pounding his fist upon an unseen door and threatening to shoot.

Manning darted across the front door to the hall. The terrorist saw him advancing and turned, aiming his handgun at the Canadian. The killer's weapon fired. So did Manning's Magnum. The contest was close.

Manning felt a sharp tug on the sleeve of his coat, but the Eagle's .357 payload punched a hole through the center of the terrorist's chest. Blood gushed from the awesome wound. The gunman's face became a mask of agony, but he somehow found the strength to keep his weapon trained on Manning.

Manning fired the .357 again and doubled the size of the terrorist's chest wound. The Rote-Abend gunman staggered in reverse and fell through an open doorway, his autoloader slipping from his fingers and crashing to the wooden floor.

The Canadian stepped farther into the corridor and checked to make sure his opponent was finished. He was. Manning went to the door that the gunman had been trying to beat down and listened. The woman whose screams he had heard was now sobbing on the other side of the door.

Gently Manning knocked, and called out in German that it was safe for the woman to come out. He was still attempting to coax her from the room, when Encizo arrived at the apartment.

"You all right?"

"Never felt better," Manning replied. "How'd you do?"

Encizo nodded at the body on the floor. "I've got his twin downstairs in the basement. Who's hiding behind the door?"

"Lady of the house, I think. She locked herself in here before the creep taking the nap there could nab her. Now she doesn't want to come out."

"Leave her be," Encizo said. "We'll send up somebody she knows." He crossed the living room to the windows leading onto the balcony and looked outside. "Oh, no!"

Manning crossed to Encizo. "What?"

The Cuban pulled back the curtain and pointed to where police cars, ambulances and a crowd of residents of Plittersdorf were gathered around Stimson Memorial Chapel. The back doors to one of the ambulances were open and a stretcher bearing a body was being lifted inside.

"It looks like they got Dieter," said Encizo.

21

When Gunther Heisler was escorted by two armed guards into Gregor Churatov's private office it was to find the Russian sitting behind his desk, diligently thumbing through the pages of a hardcover book. A plain paper jacket had been applied to the book, so Heisler was unable to read its title as he was facing Churatov's desk.

"It is most strange," Churatov said once his men had departed from the room. He handed the book to Heisler. "I have been looking through it for a long time, and it is simply not there. Tomorrow I shall file a complaint with the publisher."

Heisler leaned forward and accepted the book, opening it to the title page. He frowned. The book was a Russian-German dictionary. The terrorist closed the dictionary and set it back on the desk.

"I do not understand," he said, perplexed. "There is something missing from the book?"

"Apparently so, Herr Heisler. I looked up such words as incompetent, worthless and overpaid. Impossibly, none of the German equivalents of those words is Rote Abend. How do you explain it?''

Heisler's eyes flashed with ill-disguised anger. ''In addition to those killed the last time we spoke, Comrade Churatov, I have lost sixteen more of my people today. You will forgive me, then, if I fail to find what you have just told me amusing.''

''My comments were not intended to amuse,'' Churatov said. ''Rote Abend's dismal showing at Plittersdorf has compounded what was already a distressing failure. Your so-called terrorist army, Herr Heisler, has been publicly shamed and your soldiers have been made to look like idiots.''

''Not entirely,'' Heisler protested. ''I am told we did succeed in sending one of our adversaries to the hospital.''

''What? At a cost of sixteen lives? Preposterous. You must explain to me sometime this interesting theory of mathematics which equates sixteen deaths to one wounding. Losing sixteen for one is hardly cause to bring out the party hats and noisemakers.''

''I agree,'' Heisler said bitterly. ''This whole business involving the abduction of Karl Hahn has proved intolerably expensive. Two days ago I had more than fifty Rote-Abend members at my disposal. Now I command only a half-dozen.''

''Lamentable, but don't complain to me about it,'' advised Churatov. ''You were and have been paid handsomely for your services. This is a war we are fighting here, not some game on paper where the victims are imaginary. You should not have accepted our financial support if you were not prepared to suffer casualties.''

"Casualties are one thing," Heisler countered. "What we're dealing with is something else, something closer to wholesale slaughter. Rote Abend is not ungrateful for your financial assistance, Comrade Churatov, but the problems we have faced trying to eliminate the mysterious one-armed man and his companions have nothing to do with whether the money spent funding Rote Abend was squandered. You and I both know it was not.

"Clearly the one-armed devil and his band of killers are not textbook soldiers—they are professionals. They have outclassed my forces right from the beginning. If I had known earlier what I know now, I would have insisted that you supply us with more than a fat bank account. I would have demanded armed personnel from your camp to augment mine. You are correct when you say we are fighting a war, but up until now all of us have been prepared to fight. Evidently, in some circles money is a substitute for courage.''

One of Churatov's fake smiles touched his mouth but did not reach his eyes. "Show me your wounds, Herr Heisler. With the exception of the night Karl Hahn was kidnapped, I fail to recall any time you yourself took to the battlefield. You have allowed your people to do the dying for you.''

''Historically, it has always been the commander's burden to watch from the sidelines as his troops engage the enemy,'' Heisler said in his defense.

''If our comprehension of history is as poor as your mathematics, then I will sit out today's lesson, thank you. Yesterday does not concern me. The here and now does. Rote Abend's incompetence has necessitated a change in plans. The one-armed man you have repeatedly failed to kill is still somewhere in Bonn, and I have no intention of letting him, or his associates, interfere further. We shall, therefore, initiate a new wrinkle to the scheme of things.''

''What manner of 'new wrinkle' do you propose?''

''The longer we wait to trade Karl Hahn for Josef Roetz, the more time our opponents have to create headaches for both of us. We must make the time of the prisoner exchange work for us, not for our opponents. Your West-German authorities are expecting the exchange to occur at dawn tomorrow. I believe that time frame is no longer feasible. Consequently, I want you to inform your nation's internal security personnel that we are setting the prisoner exchange ahead by six hours. We will trade Hahn for Roetz tonight at midnight.''

''Good,'' Heisler said, reluctantly adding, ''Your idea has merit. Where shall I tell the authorities that the exchange is to be made?''

"Same as before," Churatov answered. "Overlooking Bonn in the Siebengiberge. Tell him to be there at midnight with Roetz."

"And after the exchange?" Heisler asked hopefully.

"After Josef Roetz has been returned to us, Rote Abend has our blessing to continue as originally scheduled. Will you be able to meet the new deadline?"

"Of course," Heisler assured the Russian. "We labored through the night securing the supplies necessary for the project's success. Our MRL has been fully stocked with the munitions required to produce sarin since early this morning."

The MRL Heisler referred to was a multiple rocket launcher—a vehicle-mounted frame containing tubes for launching a specified number of unguided artillery rockets. The rockets were rigged to fire individually, simultaneously or in a sequence known as ripple fire. MRLs were very effective in concentrating large volumes of a chemical agent on a target in a very short time.

"You will need to get the MRL up to the vicinity of the exchange point long before midnight," Churatov said. "You will have to set your coordinates to strike your designated targets in Bonn."

"Have no fear," Heisler said, "the targets will be set. And considering how many Rote Abend have fallen since Friday, my satisfaction at watching the MRL empty its payload will be immense.''

''And mine,'' confirmed Churatov. ''Naturally I expect all your remaining Rote-Abend members to participate in tonight's adventure. As they are aware of your plans, I doubt any of them wish to spend the night in Bonn.''

''Correct,'' Heisler said. ''Not when morning will find Bonn a city of the dead.'' He pushed back his chair and stood. ''If there is nothing else, then, I will go now to notify the authorities that they are to deliver Roetz to us by midnight.''

''Do that,'' Gregor Churatov said. ''Until later this evening, then.''

Churatov activated a button on his desk and the door to his office immediately opened, admitting the same two armed guards who had previously brought Heisler to the room. Now they escorted him out.

No sooner had Heisler left than Churatov went downstairs for a brief conversation with Karl Hahn. As before, and to the Soviet's frustration, Hahn exhibited no outward signs of fear, nor did he press Churatov for any information other than what he chose to divulge.

''We have decided to orchestrate your release earlier than anticipated,'' the Russian said after entering Hahn's cell.

''Is that so?'' Hahn said dryly.

"Yes," Churatov confirmed. "If all goes well you will be a free man at midnight."

"Assuming you are given Josef Roetz," Hahn stated.

"Oh, we will get Roetz, all right. Your BND will see to that. I am certain they have no desire to see you die. We will get Roetz; they will get Karl Hahn. Both sides will be happy. I thought you would appreciate knowing of the change in plans."

"And I do," Hahn said. "But not for any reason you might think."

Churatov could not resist asking, "Why, then?"

"It will give me time to pack."

Churatov shook his head at Hahn's indifference and left, locking the door behind him.

The lights in the cell went out and Hahn sat alone with his thoughts. Not for a second did he believe Churatov had altered the timetable for the exchange without just cause. Beneath his controlled exterior, Gregor Churatov was running scared.

In Hahn's mind there was only one explanation for the Russian's change in plans: Phoenix Force. Hahn knew his Stony-Man friends were doing everything within their power to pull him out of this mess in one piece. Ultimately, though, the success or failure of their mission depended upon the delivery of Josef Roetz.

And how was that going to happen? Although Phoenix Force was big on accomplishing seemingly impossible tasks, even they were going to have difficulty raising the dead.

22

"How goes it?" asked Dieter Beck.

"That's what we should be asking you," Manning said. "How does your shoulder feel?"

Dressed in a hospital gown, Beck was sitting up in bed, his back propped up by a stack of pillows. He shifted uncomfortably at the mention of his wound.

"It aches like hell," the Canadian's BKA friend reported. "And the doctors promise me that by tomorrow it will hurt even more. I must look on the bright side, they say. The Rote-Abend bullet could have killed me."

"How is Frau Beck taking your injury?" inquired Katz.

"As I expected she would. She's upset that I was shot, but relieved I'm alive. Annette is a strong woman. With my line of work she has to be." He changed position again. "Chief Superintendent Mader was in to check on me just before you arrived."

"We know," Manning said. "He asked us to wait outside while he spoke to you."

Beck nodded. "Mader told me the BKA received a telephone call from Rote Abend while I was in surgery. It would seem the pressure we've put on them since Friday evening has affected their plans. The terrorists have switched the time for trading the prisoners from dawn tomorrow to midnight tonight."

"Less than seven hours from now," McCarter said.

Beck regarded Manning. "Have you come up with anything?"

"We're working on it," Manning replied. "We still don't know where the prisoner exchange is to take place."

"And we won't know until later this evening," Beck said. "Rote Abend wants to keep us in the dark until the last possible moment, to prevent us from preparing some kind of trap for them."

"Which we're somehow going to have to do if we want to save Hahn," James concluded.

Encizo shrugged. "How do we do that without Josef Roetz along for the ride? Once Rote Abend sees the trade is a bust, they'll kill Hahn for sure."

Beck sighed wearily. "You're absolutely right. I would judge at least seventy-five percent of Rote Abend's members have been eliminated over the past few days. With such heavy losses Gunther Heisler and his friends will be more unstable than ever. It won't take much to provoke them into killing Hahn. At this point, what do they have to lose?"

"A dead geezer named Josef Roetz," McCarter grumbled. "They've lost him already and don't even know it."

"Maybe." Beck paused and stared at the cockney. Then he smiled and went on. "Then again, maybe not." Suddenly he kicked back his covers and, holding his wounded shoulder stiffly, swung his feet over the side of the bed to the floor.

"Where do you think you're going?" asked Manning.

"Help me find my clothes," the BKA man said. "There's so much to do and so little time to do it in. You must help me get out of here."

"You've thought of something that might help us?" Katz questioned.

"Perhaps," Beck said. "There may be a way we can give Rote Abend what they want."

James frowned. "How's that? Roetz is dead."

"I know he is," Beck said, "but did you ever see his photograph?"

RICHARD WASSER PAINSTAKINGLY fine-tuned his latest masterpiece. "Steady now. In a few moments I will be finished. I have done my part. Now you must do yours. All it takes is confidence."

Josef Roetz, or at least someone who resembled him, looked in the mirror and shook his head in disbelief. "It will never work," he said.

"Sure it will," James said, looking from the photograph of Roetz in his hands to the face in the mirror. "You're the spitting image of Roetz."

"You're mad," the man with Roetz's face said, pointing to his reflection. "This wouldn't fool Roetz's mum."

"We don't need to fool his mother," Manning countered. "She won't be there."

McCarter turned away from the mirror. "It wouldn't fool her if she was."

"Bitte," Wasser admonished. "You must hold still."

The wiry Wasser was one of his country's foremost makeup artists. Pulled from the set of a film entitled, in English, *The Cold French Fry*, Wasser had been flown to Bonn on an emergency flight from Munich. Sworn to secrecy, he had spent the four hours since his arrival transforming David McCarter's face into a reasonable facsimile of that of the late Josef Roetz.

With a combination of several foundation shades Wasser altered the tone of McCarter's skin, aging the cockney by twenty-five years. A bump on Roetz's nose was duplicated on McCarter's with a lump of derma wax, expertly applied and blended in until it was impossible to tell that the bump was false.

Wrinkles in the forehead and pouches under the eyes were created with liquid latex. The contours of the Briton's face were changed to match Roetz's by the application of tints of soft shadow. Finally, when

Wasser was satisfied with his work, he lightly dusted McCarter's features with face powder.

Wasser brushed away the excess powder, then handed McCarter a towel. "Here. Cover your face."

"It'll take more than that to hide a botched job," the Londoner warned.

Wasser ignored the remark. "The towel is to protect your eyes while I spray your hair."

"I knew that," McCarter insisted, putting the towel to its intended use. When Wasser set down the spray can a few minutes later McCarter's hair was a dull silver-gray.

"Gentlemen," the makeup artist announced, "I give you Josef Roetz." He whipped the towel from McCarter's face and stepped back. "Well, what to you think?"

"I want my money back," McCarter said.

Dieter Beck stepped forward to congratulate Wasser. "Splendid, Herr Wasser. I have seen Josef Roetz in person, and now, through your expertise, I see him again. *Wunderbar!*"

"You've done a fantastic job," Katz added. "Thank you for making yourself available to us on such short notice."

"I was happy to be of service," Wasser said, beginning to take down the photographs of Josef Roetz that were taped around the mirror in front of McCarter. "Of course, my subjects are usually a little more cooperative."

"They have to be, don't they?" McCarter said. "One cross word to you and they'd go before the cameras looking like Quasimodo."

"Pay no attention to Herr Black," Manning apologized for McCarter. "He's this way with everyone."

Wasser closed his tubes of greasepaint and containers of powder, tightened the lid on his bottle of liquid latex and recapped all the eye liners and shading pencils he had used. Then he placed the items inside the sturdy metal box that he had brought with him from Munich. Last to be put away were soft brushes of assorted sizes and the aerosol can of gray hair spray.

"So," Wasser announced, closing and securing the lid on his makeup kit, then picking it up by its handle, "that is all I can do. Even given more time I could not have done better. An artist cannot paint when the canvas is not primed. Still, I hope my work satisfies the audience for which it is intended."

"I am certain it will pass the test admirably," Beck assured Wasser, escorting the makeup technician to the door. "Will you be spending the evening in Bonn?"

"No, it is back to München, I'm afraid. I start work early in the morning, hours before the actors set foot on the movie set."

"Permit me to walk you to Hauptwachtmeister Conradt's desk, then," Beck said. "He will drive you to the airport."

Phoenix Force, including McCarter, thanked Wasser and said goodbye. Beck, favoring his injured shoulder but getting about well in spite of his discomfort and the restrictive bandages, took Wasser to catch his ride back to the airport. "Come on," Encizo encouraged McCarter. "Admit it. Herr Wasser did a great job on you."

"Ask me again after midnight." McCarter sipped Coke through a straw. "This makeup itches like hell."

"Dieter's idea of sending for Wasser was inspired," Katz told the Englishman. "In spite of your objections, David, Wasser has given you the face of Josef Roetz. I could easily mistake you for the spy. We're lucky you and Roetz are fairly close in height and weight. If we had to resort to body padding or heel lifts to complete the disguise, your freedom of movement could be restricted."

"I know," the British battle ace agreed. "And after Heisler and his pals discover I'm not the real McCoy, I've got a feeling I'll need all the freedom of movement I can get."

James checked his watch. "It's just after eleven. Rote Abend is running this horse race right down to the wire."

"If Dieter's estimate is correct," Manning said, "and we have killed off most of Rote Abend's members, then Heisler's terrorists probably won't be our only opposition at the exchange site."

"I've thought of that," Katz said. "And you're right. Gunther Heisler may be center stage for the prisoner trade, but there are bound to be Soviet forces hovering in the background. How large the Russian contingent will be is anybody's guess, but we'll definitely have them to deal with.

"Also," the Israeli colonel added, "there's something else to think about—namely, the cylinder of isopropanol in the Red-Evening weapons cache we found at the deserted factory Friday night. We don't know if Rote Abend has mixed the component with a catalyst and methyl phosphonyl difluoride to produce the nerve agent sarin."

"Do you think they plan to use it after the exchange is made?" Encizo asked.

Katz shrugged. "I don't know. Because of us, Rote Abend has to be carrying one hell of a big chip on their shoulder. We've hit them and hit them hard. Revenge is a powerful motive. If they didn't have a reason to use the sarin before, we've certainly presented them with one now."

"Okay," McCarter said flatly. "Where does Karl fit into all this? I mean, if we're going through with the exchange, and he's coming this way and I'm going that, what do we say when we pass each other besides 'bread and butter'?"

"I hope," Katz answered, "that Karl will know or at least suspect by now that we are here in Bonn to help him. Even if he doesn't, once he sees us at the exchange site, he'll know what to do.

"When we send you toward Heisler, David, you will be armed, something Rote Abend is not likely to suspect. You will also carry an extra gun for Karl. You be the judge. When you feel the time is right, draw your weapon and open fire. The surprise of the man Rote Abend thinks is Josef Roetz shooting at them should buy us the time we'll require to launch a successful attack."

"During which time I pass Hahn a gun and we all live happily ever after." McCarter sighed and resisted the overwhelming urge to scratch his nose. "I've always been muggins for a soft sell, Katz. And here I thought this was going to be complicated and dangerous. Silly me."

"We'll pull it off," Katz said, confidently. "Until then, try to relax."

"Impossible." The East Ender laughed. "I'd have a Player's, but with all this grease on my face, I'm afraid my head would explode."

The door to the room opened then as Dieter Beck returned. Under his good arm he carried a flat cardboard box. "It looks like show time," he said immediately, setting the box down. "Chief Superintendent Mader just received a call from Gunther Heisler."

"And?" Manning prompted.

"And," the BKA man continued, "we now know where the prisoner exchange will be held. Josef Roetz is to be traded for Karl Hahn in the Siebengibirge."

"The Seven Hills." Manning repeated the location in English for those who did not speak German. "They overlook Bonn from the other side of the Rhine, don't they, Dieter?"

"Correct," Beck affirmed. "There's a nature park in the Siebengibirge, and it's there, in a clearing Heisler has designated, that the trade will be made."

"What are Heisler's specific instructions?" Katz asked.

"Pretty much as anticipated," Beck told him. "Only one vehicle, the one carrying Roetz, is to come to the exchange site. A van or minibus is acceptable, but nothing larger. Escort vehicles of any kind will not be permitted. The delivery vehicle with Roetz in it is to arrive precisely at midnight.

"No more than three BKA agents, including the driver, may accompany Roetz to the site. Gunther Heisler says he expects the BKA men to be armed, but warns strongly against using any weapons before, during or after the exchange.

"The vehicle is to drive to the edge of a popular picnic area and park. Roetz and two of the BKA operatives are to leave the vehicle, while the driver remains at the wheel.

"Once outside the delivery vehicle, Roetz and his guards are to proceed to the middle of a chalked-out circle directly across from a brick barbecue that is on the site. Heisler and one Rote-Abend terrorist will be standing with Hahn inside a similar circle on the barbecue's other side. Verification will be made at that time that Roetz and Hahn are indeed Roetz and Hahn. Then the exchange will take place."

"How will the verification be conducted?" James asked.

"With a high-intensity hand-held spotlight," Beck replied. "Heisler's spotlight will be operated by the driver of his delivery vehicle. Our driver has permission to do the same."

"And after the trade is completed?" Encizo quizzed.

"Both parties will return peacefully to their respective vehicles and drive out of the park. Our vehicle is to go back in the direction from which it came."

"Neat, isn't it?" McCarter said.

"Heisler warned Mader that any deviation from the rules he has laid down for the trade will be considered just cause for terminating the agreement—and for terminating Hahn."

"Bingo! Let's do it," McCarter said anxiously, standing and pointing to the cardboard box Beck had brought into the room. "What's all this then?"

Beck answered with a smile. "A present for you."

23

Phoenix Force and Dieter Beck rode in the Mercedes-Benz nine-passenger minibus from Bonn into the Sie-bengibirge, which looked down on the city. Since their departure from BKA headquarters twenty minutes earlier, the rain that had plagued the area off and on all weekend long started to fall heavily again. As they drove into the hills raindrops the size of small eggs pelted their windshield, and cold winds buffeted the van from all sides.

The West-German minibus had been specially customized for use by the BKA, with windows of bulletproof glass, built-in armor plating and wheels that could withstand anything short of a direct confrontation with a land mine.

Manning was at the wheel, with Beck temporarily riding shotgun and the rest of the Stony-Man team occupying seats to the rear. The mood inside the van was one of quiet contemplation. Even McCarter was pensive. Phoenix Force had come to Bonn to help a friend whose life was threatened by murderous savages. The success or failure of their mission was about to be determined.

Phoenix Force expected a war in the Siebengibirge and were armed accordingly. In addition to a healthy supply of fragmentation and incendiary grenades, each warrior was prepared, with his individual choice of weapons, to make life hell for Gunther Heisler and his band of fanatics.

Rafael Encizo's battle gear began with his Heckler and Koch MP-5 machine pistol. The H&K dynamo was fitted with a detachable box magazine of thirty 9 mm parabellum rounds and had a silencer attached to its barrel. Additional firepower for the Havana hotshot was provided by the S&W M-59 autoloader worn on his hip and a Walther PPK that used .380 caliber bullets, in a shoulder rig.

Yakov Katzenelenbogen's Uzi submachine gun had supported the Israeli commando through numerous encounters against enemy forces in the past and was fitted now with a noise suppressor. Katz's backup piece was a SIG-Sauer P-226.

For long-range capability and superior stopping power, Gary Manning depended on his .357 Magnum, which he carried in a shoulder holster. Because he would be one of the two men delivering "Josef Roetz" to the exchange site, he was also armed with a H&K MP-5, the weapon of choice of West Germany's security forces.

Calvin James's equipment would have set an airport's metal detectors into overload. He wore a .357

Colt Python Old West-style on his hip, and also carried with his G-96 Boot 'n Belt knife, a Colt Commander in shoulder rig, a S&W M-76 chatterbox and a Ring Airfoil Grenade launcher.

Engineered by DARPA during the height of the Vietnam conflict and then abandoned in a jungle of red tape and bureaucratic ignorance, the RAG launcher's magazine held five 53 mm rounds. Unlike an M-79, whose 40 mm minibombs traveled to their target in a sharp trajectory, the aeroballistic design of the RAG's doughnut-shaped projectiles enabled the launcher to be fired like a rifle. Each of the RAG rounds could effectively dispatch a target up to forty-two hundred feet away.

David McCarter's ill-fitting raincoat concealed a variety of firearms. Besides his Ingram MAC-10 and Browning Hi-Power, the Londoner wore a .38 Special Charter Arms snubby revolver tucked away in a holster at the small of his back. Inside McCarter's raincoat was a pocket where the weapon he hoped to be able to pass to Hahn was hidden. The weapon was an Ingram M-11 SMG, sometimes referred to as the MAC-10's little brother.

Because Dieter Beck's shoulder wound prevented his using more than one hand to fire a gun, the BKA agent had armed himself with a Walther P-5 automatic. If it was needed, a duplicate of Beck's handgun could be pulled into action from a recessed area of the Merc van's dashboard.

Manning took the minibus around a curve and the road began to climb. "How much farther?" he asked.

"About one kilometer to go," Beck answered. "Then we will be at the picnic grounds where Heisler is supposed to meet us."

"Bloody fine night for a picnic," McCarter complained. "Much more rain and Karl and I will have to swim toward each other to complete the exchange."

"There's been nobody but us on this road for at least two klicks," Encizo commented.

"That's 'cause all the decent people in the world are dry at home in their beds," James decided.

Manning applied pressure to the brakes and brought the minibus to a halt. "We'd better switch places now, Dieter," he told his friend. "Rote Abend could have sentries posted up ahead, and we don't want them getting suspicious. You take us the rest of the way in." He and Beck traded places.

"It's time we were getting out of sight," Katz said to James. While Beck brought them nearer to their goal, the Israeli and American both left the comfort of their seats to sit on the van's floor.

The arrival was perfectly timed. At exactly midnight Beck drove the Mercedes-Benz van onto the Siebengibirge picnic grounds. Grateful for the van's power steering, he took the Merc into a tight turn that ended when the minibus's side panel door was directly across from a large brick barbecue. Beck killed the Merc's engine.

"Break a leg!" Beck smiled to McCarter. "Isn't that what you say to an actor before he goes on stage?"

"Search me," McCarter responded.

Manning pressed his face against the window and squinted through the rainfall to see beyond the barbecue to the other side of the picnic area.

"Okay," the Canadian announced. "I can see them. They're in a van pretty much like ours. Wait, hold on. The door of their vehicle just opened and one, two, now three people have just climbed out. Numbers one and three both have guns trained on number two, so he must be Karl." Manning swiveled in his seat and looked back at McCarter. "That's our cue, Herr Roetz. Knock 'em dead."

"Ja, ja," the cockney answered.

Manning sent a quick glance at Encizo and grinned. "I'll handle Heisler if he starts getting talkative."

Encizo, who barely spoke ten words of German, answered Manning's statement with a grin of his own. "No shit."

"Let's do it," Manning said.

His H&K MP-5 strapped over his shoulder and in plain sight, Manning opened his door and stepped out into the rain. He turned, pressed down on the handle of the van's sliding door, then pulled it open far enough to allow McCarter and Encizo to get out, but not so far as to reveal Katz and James hiding inside on the minibus floor.

Training his machine pistol on McCarter, Manning motioned him out and moved back. Immediately

McCarter joined Manning outside the van, quickly followed by Encizo.

Manning waited for Encizo to close the van's sliding door, then together he and his Cuban friend led McCarter at gunpoint to the circle where Heisler had instructed them to stand. Across the picnic grounds the three men Manning had watched leaving the Rote-Abend van were going through the same motions.

"Good evening!" Gunther Heisler's powerful voice cut through the pounding rain. "You have brought us Josef Roetz?"

"If you have brought us Karl Hahn," Manning replied in flawless German.

"We shall both see," Heisler said. "Are you ready with your spotlight?"

"We are," the Canadian answered. "Whenever you are ready."

"Now!"

Simultaneously the high-intensity spotlight attached to the terrorists' vehicle and the one operated by Beck in the BKA van were turned on, bathing both groups of three figures in a silver-white glow. Avoiding looking directly into the Rote Abend's spotlight, the three Phoenix-Force warriors at once identified the man standing between Gunther Heisler and an older man they did not recognize. True professional that he was, Hahn gave no indication that he recognized the Phoenix-Force men opposite him.

Once confirmation was made by Phoenix Force, they held their breath to see if Richard Wasser's makeup job on McCarter would pass its crucial test. Manning's trigger finger rubbed back and forth over his thumb. Encizo toughed out the wait by blinking raindrops from his eyes. McCarter, face expressionless, passively portrayed the prisoner he was supposed to be, while wishing he had not been rude to Wasser.

Time dragged on for all three men. Rote Abend's spotlight seemed to have been trained on them for an eternity. At last Heisler called out in a satisfied voice, "Very well. You have brought us Josef Roetz."

"And you have brought Karl Hahn," Manning stated.

"Good," Heisler said. "Send Roetz to me, and you shall get Hahn. Then we will all return to our vehicles and go our separate ways. At the count of three let the exchange begin."

Heisler counted out loud. After he reached three, Hahn and McCarter started walking slowly toward each other.

"The exchange has begun," Beck informed Katz and James in the back of the van. "Get ready."

"Got it," James whispered, holding his RAG launcher in his left hand, while gripping the van's sliding door handle in his right. "Just give me the word."

"This is going to be close," Katz said.

McCarter and Hahn were within ten feet of each other. The expression on Hahn's face told McCarter that Richard Wasser's work had not fooled the BND agent. The brick barbecue was directly ahead. It was there he would give the M-11 to—

Something slammed into McCarter's chest, throwing him to the muddy ground. A sudden crack of rifle fire accompanied his fall, but the stunned Briton was oblivious of the sound. Pain flooded his chest and his world began to go black.

"Shit!" Manning shouted. "They shot him!"

No sooner had McCarter hit the ground than Hahn, too, threw himself onto the muddy earth. Hahn grabbed McCarter's coat and began dragging him behind the brick barbecue, while the air about them was filled with destruction.

Manning and Encizo opened fire with their MP-5 machine pistols, at the same time diving for cover. Both Phoenix pros caught a glimpse of Heisler and his companion doing the same, then the Canadian and the Cuban launched their firepower at a wave of screaming terrorists attacking in a frontal assault.

Manning caught the Red-Evening hood in the head with a H&K headache that scrambled the killer's brains. Encizo drilled a pair of holes in the stomach of the next terrorist in line. Shrieking from the fire ripping through his abdomen, the gutshot killer clutched his bleeding belly and collapsed face-first in a deep puddle, where he drowned.

Dieter Beck had no need to signal Calvin James or Yakov Katzenelenbogen that it was time for action. Throwing open the minibus's sliding door, the guy from Chicago leaped out into the rain. He braced the stock of the RAG launcher against his shoulder, aimed and fired in a single smooth motion, sending the RAG round straight at the Rote-Abend van. James corrected his aim and fired again, this time at the herd of bad guys attacking Manning and Encizo.

The first 53 mm grenade hit the enemy's van and the entire vehicle erupted in an earth-shattering explosion. Twisted metal and burning body parts flew through the air. The second RAG grenade struck precisely where James wanted, and three more Red-Evening terrorists disintegrated in a blinding flash of heat and light.

The flaming wreckage of the terrorists' van illuminated the trees surrounding the picnic grounds and revealed to James a pair of snipers hiding high among the branches of a tall pine tree. James zeroed in on the duo without hesitation, firing the Ring Airfoil Grenade launcher's final three rounds.

Like miniature meteors of doom, the triple dose of 53 mm airfoil grenades reduced the evergreen to sap and splinters. The airborne snipers windmilled and screamed their way below as James unslung the RAG launcher in favor of his M-76.

Katz had been about to climb out of the BKA van, when a series of metallic punches thudded into the minibus's armor-plated body near the back.

"They're attacking from behind!" Beck shouted, sliding across to the driver's side of the van again. He shoved his Walther automatic out the partially opened window and into the face of a Russian assassin trying to climb inside.

Katz added his fire to Beck's as another two Soviet gunmen prepared to open up their weapons on the van. The Israeli got there first, hosing down all three of the astonished terrorists in a shower of Uzi lead. Twitching and dancing as the slugs bit through their flesh, they sank to their knees and died. Katz redirected his aim as two more Russian killers came at him and Beck out of the dark.

WITH BULLETS BLAZING all around them, Karl Hahn managed to get McCarter's body behind the barrier of the brick barbecue. In the light of the burning wreckage of the Rote-Abend van, he could see the entry wound on McCarter's raincoat, a neat round hole over the Londoner's heart. However, no blood was visible.

Hahn knew McCarter had to be packing some kind of arsenal underneath his rain gear, and was not disappointed when he tore open the coat. Most prominent among the Briton's assortment of weapons was McCarter's Ingram MAC-10 subgun.

"Help yourself," McCarter said, groaning as he propped himself up with his arm.

Hahn looked at him in surprise. "I thought your number had been called."

"What's the big hurry? I'm not about to cash in my chips yet." McCarter tapped the bullet hole in his raincoat. "Matthews body armor. A friend of Manning's with the BKA had me put it on before we came here tonight." He poked his finger through the hole. "Good move, right?"

Before Hahn could answer an enterprising Communist killer came leaping over the top of the barbecue with a scream of triumph, landing with a crash on McCarter and his BND ally. McCarter collapsed beneath the weight of the Russian, while Hahn was thrown to his back. The Soviet's machine pistol went flying from his grip.

The killer, whom Hahn recognized as one of Gregor Churatov's henchmen, seized what he thought was an opportunity to stomp the West German's face into jelly. But Hahn's hands lashed out and caught the descending foot, holding it as he arched himself off the ground and planted his own booted extremity between the Russian's legs.

Hahn's adversary screamed in pain the second Hahn's foot connected. Hahn rolled out of the way as the Communist hood fell, but not fast enough to evade the beefy hands reaching out to strangle him. Hahn's fingers clawed at the earth and came up with two handfuls of sticky mud, which he pressed into the Russian's eyes. The hands throttling Hahn relaxed their torturous grip. Hahn pushed with all his might against his opponent's chest.

Shielding his injured testicles with one hand, wiping mud from his eyes with the other, the Russian staggered backward to his feet, directly into the path of the sizzling lead Manning and Encizo sent rocketing his way. The killer collapsed, dying in agony.

Crouching, Hahn returned to the protection of the brick barbecue, where McCarter was waiting.

"Here," said the cockney, reaching into his raincoat's secret pocket for the M-11 SMG. "I brought this for you."

GREGOR CHURATOV LIFTED his face from the mud and warily looked from left to right. The world was on fire; at least, his half of it was. Heisler's van was destroyed and his snipers were gone, blown to pieces through a series of teeth-rattling explosions. Churatov shuddered. Most of his men were dead or dying. Cries of the mortally wounded filled the air.

Churatov swore to himself. Damn Heisler's Rote-Abend incompetence, anyway. His snipers had succeeded in killing Josef Roetz, but what difference did that make now? The world was falling apart and it was all Heisler's fault. If the flimsy excuse for a terrorist leader had done his job properly, none of this would have happened. But, no. That miserable bastard Heisler had to ruin everything with one tactical blunder after another.

Right then nothing would have pleased Churatov more than placing a gun against Heisler's skull and pulling the trigger. Such pleasures, he knew, would have to wait, because the first item on his agenda was to save his ass, and to do that he had to sneak away from the picnic grounds unseen.

Clutching his H&K machine pistol for dear life, Churatov crawled across the muddy ground on his stomach toward a row of pine trees nearby. He froze and played dead as one of the enemy, a black man wielding an SMG, entered his line of vision.

The Russian cursed under his breath. The man was all that stood between him and escape. What was he to do? Then his enemy looked in another direction and Churatov relaxed. He had not been spotted. He was safe. Already the man was turning away. When he had turned his back completely, Churatov would shoot him from behind, and the road to freedom would be clear.

Churatov raised his MP-5 to fire, but reconsidered his plan when a lightning bolt of pain stitched a course along his ribs. He coughed and spit blood. His insides were cooking. His gun was too heavy. He dropped it.

Using the last of his strength, Churatov squinted up to see the face of his executioner. His vision grew dim and he carried the man's image to his grave. Of all people, Josef Roetz. Impossible. Damn Heisler....

The last of the Russians assaulting the BKA van had been repelled and eliminated by Katz and Beck. Manning and Encizo were shooting it out with a pocket of die-hards too dumb to know they were beaten. James and McCarter were working their way back to the brick barbecue area; Hahn's cover fire was helping them get there. Meanwhile the continuing downpour had doused the flames of the RAG-blown enemy van, reducing the vehicle to a twisted pile of smoldering rubble.

"It appears our efforts have paid off," Dieter Beck concluded as he directed the minibus's spotlight to encompass a larger area. "Rote Abend has been defeated and Karl Hahn has been saved."

As the spotlight swept over a line of evergreens bordering the picnic grounds Katz called out to Beck, "Hold the light."

Beck did as instructed and focused the spotlight on the area Katz designated. "What did you see?"

"Someone moving in back of one of the trees," Katz replied. "I'm not sure."

"I saw nothing," Beck said, squinting. "Perhaps it was the rain and shadows playing tricks on your eyes."

"Perhaps," Katz said, unconvinced. "Let's find out."

The Israeli leaned from the van and sent a volley of Uzi lead spraying into the trees. Then he aimed slightly lower and repeated the process. A lone figure suddenly darted from behind a large pine. For a millisecond the person was framed in the spotlight, and then disappeared into the trees.

"Mein Gott!" exclaimed Beck. "It was Heisler!"

But Katz was already out of the minibus and chasing after his foe.

GUNTHER HEISLER CHARGED through the Siebengibirge's pine forest with an agility that surprised even him. He held no illusions; Rote Abend was history.

What he had seen back at the exchange site told him that none of his comrades lived. He was the sole survivor.

Churatov and his Russian clowns had fared no better. All their talk of superiority on the battlefield amounted to a lot of hot air. When push came to shove the Communists died as quickly as Rote Abend.

Heisler was unafraid. He had no reason for fear. His enemies had lost their chance to stop him, and would pay dearly for their failure. They were ignorant fools, casting themselves as conquering heroes, but they were wrong. They were losers, not winners as they would soon discover.

Heisler smiled. He would show them. In a few short minutes he would activate the MRL, sending more than enough of the nerve agent sarin to blanket Bonn with a different kind of rain.

The pine trees thinned out and Heisler forced himself to run faster. He broke out of the forest into the clearing where the MRL was mounted on a heavy-duty flatbed truck. His smile split his face and he laughed out loud in triumph as he hurried toward the MRL. His enemies might have won the battle, but the war belonged to Gunther Heisler.

''Heisler!''

The Rote-Abend founder turned at the calling of his name and saw his one-armed nemesis rush into the clearing.

''You!'' Heisler spit in disbelief.

"Who else?" Katz asked, recognizing in the darkness the outline of a BM-21 Multiple Rocket Launcher behind Heisler. The firing tubes of the Soviet-made MRL were aimed in the direction of Bonn.

"No!" Heisler screamed, recovering from the shock of seeing the man responsible for so many Rote-Abend deaths. "No!"

The terrorist leader snapped up his H&K machine pistol to fire. Katz's noise-suppressed Uzi spoke first. A dozen 9 mm rounds hammered into Heisler's abdomen. He whimpered and slipped to the carpet of mud at his feet.

Five minutes later a rain-soaked Katz returned to the picnic-ground site of the prisoner exchange to find his Stony-Man teammates, as well as Karl Hahn and Dieter, mopping up after the fight.

As Katz approached Manning said, "Dieter told us you went after Heisler."

"And caught him," Katz informed everyone. "I put him to sleep in front of an MRL aimed at Bonn. He was going to use the sarin." He glanced around. "How'd you make out?"

James grinned. "The other side lost."

Hahn came forward and extended his left hand to Katz. "Thank you."

"The pleasure was mine," Katz said, shaking Hahn's hand. "What do you say we get out of the rain?" Katz held up his prosthesis. "I wouldn't want this thing to rust."

EPILOGUE

Early Monday morning Phoenix Force was summoned to BKA headquarters and ushered into the office of Chief Superintendent Gerald Mader. Also invited to attend the meeting were Karl Hahn and Dieter Beck.

"You men are to be congratulated," Mader said once everyone was assembled. "No one likes to admit a mistake, but after your remarkable performance in the Siebengibirge last night, you leave me no choice.

"Had I succeeded in expelling you from the Federal Republic of Germany on Saturday evening, as I'd wished, I would have regretted that decision for the rest of my life. And judging from the nasty business Rote Abend had planned for the city, that might not have been too long."

"We did what we had to do," Katz stated honestly.

Mader beamed. "Herr Hahn is a fortunate man to have such friends. For that matter, all of Bonn is fortunate. Because of your efforts to rescue Herr Hahn, a vile terrorist organization has been obliterated and countless innocent lives spared a horrible death.

"Bonn will be forever in your debt, gentlemen. I cannot image how we could repay you, but if we can ever be of help to you, do not hesitate to ask."

"Well," Katz said, "now that you mention it ..."

Mader was all smiles. "Yes?"

"There is something you could do," Katz said.

"Name it."

"I would like you to put what you've just told us into a letter that we could take with us. In case we have some explaining to do back home. Would that be possible?"

"Of course," Mader replied. "Is that all?"

James coughed.

"Oh, yes, one more thing," Katz added. "Before we leave Bonn, could we arrange to see where Beethoven was born?"

4 FREE BOOKS
1 FREE GIFT
NO RISK
NO OBLIGATION
NO KIDDING

SPECIAL LIMITED-TIME OFFER

Mail to **Gold Eagle Reader Service**

In the U.S.	In Canada
901 Fuhrmann Blvd.	P.O. Box 609
P.O. Box 1394	Fort Erie, Ont.
Buffalo, N.Y. 14240-1394	L2A 9Z9

YEAH! Rush me 4 free Gold Eagle novels and my free mystery bonus. Then send me 6 brand-new novels every other month as they come off the presses. Bill me at the low price of just $14.95— a 13% saving off the retail price. There are no shipping, handling or other hidden costs. There is no minimum number of books I must buy. I can always return a shipment and cancel at any time. Even if I never buy another book from Gold Eagle, the 4 free novels and the mystery bonus are mine to keep forever.

Name _____ (PLEASE PRINT) _____

Address _____ Apt. No. _____

City _____ State/Prov. _____ Zip/Postal Code _____

Signature (If under 18, parent or guardian must sign)

This offer is limited to one order per household and not valid to present subscribers. Price is subject to change.

166-BPM-BP6F